Norval Clyne

Ballads from Scottish History

Norval Clyne

Ballads from Scottish History

ISBN/EAN: 9783742899507

Manufactured in Europe, USA, Canada, Australia, Japa

Cover: Foto ©Andreas Hilbeck / pixelio.de

Manufactured and distributed by brebook publishing software
(www.brebook.com)

Norval Clyne

Ballads from Scottish History

CONTENTS.

———◆——

BALLADS FROM SCOTTISH HISTORY.

I.

ST. COLUMBA.

In the history of Scotland during the first ten centuries of our era, the occurrences best authenticated are chiefly those which mark the progress of the Christian church, and the greatest name is Columba. Born in 521, nearly a hundred years after the death of St. Ninian the apostle of the Southern Picts, and preaching the gospel to the Northern Picts while the aged St. Kentigern was labouring as a bishop among the Britons of Strath-Clyde, Columba was destined to extend and complete the work of both, by his own unwearied exertions, and the judicious employment of numerous assistant missionaries and teachers. On the father's side he was of the royal line of Ulster, and his mother was the descendant of a princely house in Leinster. The purity of his childhood and youth

B

and the careful training he then received, admirably
fitted him for the holy work that was before him as
an evangelist among the Northern Picts, and the
head of the Family of Iona. In 563, several years
after his ordination as a presbyter, he left Ireland
with twelve disciples, having obtained from his
kinsman Conal, king of the Dalriadic Scots, a grant
of the "Isle of Druids," one of the smallest of the
Hebrides, but in after ages to be worthily distinguished as " I—the Island." Of its other names,
that of " I-colm-kill," though directly connecting it
with "Columba of the Cells," does not awaken our
emotion like the music of "Iona—the Holy Isle."
To use the words of a recent historian. "The first
task of St. Columba, after taking possession of the
island, was to erect a monastery and a church.
These buildings were exceedingly humble. The
church was probably of hewn timber, thatched with
reeds, like that erected at Lindisfarne by Bishop
Finan, after the manner of the Scots, as described by
Bede. The monastic buildings were of a still more
unpretending kind, as is implied in the whole narrative of Adamnan. They were, no doubt, of the same
character with those which are known to have existed
in Ireland at that time, contrasting remarkably
with the magnificent structures of after ages. The

glory of those early buildings was within."—(Grub's
Ecclesiastical History of Scotland.) St. Columba
died after midnight, on Sunday 9th June 597, in
his 76th year, and was buried in the island. Two
very early lives of the saint are extant, one written
by Cumin, sixth abbot of Iona, and the other by
Adamnan, who was the eighth abbot, having been
elected to the office in 679. The lives are printed
in Pinkerton's "Vitæ Antiquæ Sanctorum in Scotia."
Both writers had conversed with men who had repeatedly seen their great predecessor. The interesting occurrences attending the close of Columba's
life, and referred to in the following verses—the
forewarning he received of the hour of his departure,
his prediction of the future glory of Iona, and his
death before the altar—are minutely detailed in
Adamnan's work, from the information of those who
were then present. He thus concludes his biography
of the holy presbyter :—" Though he lived in this
small and remote island in the extremity of the
British ocean, his name and reputation are spread,
and his sanctity honoured, not only through all
Britain and Ireland, but even through Spain and
Gaul, and the renown of his sanctity has also pene-
trated beyond the Apennine Hills into Italy, and
into the city of Rome itself, the head and chief of

all other cities." So wrote his successor in the seventh century. In the nineteenth, how much farther might we not continue this climax of eulogy! It is enough to say, that wherever the faith of Christ is preached, the memory of the Saint of Iona is had in honour; and, as a late instance of this, the first edifice consecrated for Christian worship, west of the Mississippi, and north of the Falls of St. Anthony, among a savage Indian tribe, is the Church of St. Columba.

I.

St. Columba.

Midst the shadows of the past,
    Bright and full one form appears,
In the glory that shall last,
    Crowned with seventy stainless years.
Where yon ocean's waters sever
    Isle from isle, Columba see !
Distant far in time, but ever
    Present to our love is he ;
Standing on Iona's shore,
Named with him for evermore.

In the quenchless light of God,
    Shining from the happier West,
Scotland's farthest glens he trod,
    Stained with error's rites unblest.
On he journeyed, ne'er to falter,
    Strong with fasting, bold with prayer,
Forth against each pagan altar
    Words of truth and doom to bear ;
Hallowing with Christian vows
Temples arched with forest boughs.

Bold and wise, the holy man
    Won to truth the Pictish race,
Till the ancient waters ran
    Newly flowing founts of grace.
Where the river, rippling faintly,
    Mirrored brightly rock and tree,
There Columba, mild and saintly,
    Welcomed heavenward bond and free,
Laved in healing water thrice,
Grace-born heirs of Paradise.

In the fading light of eve,
    On Iona's slope he stands :
Gently break the waves that heave
    Sighing round its lonely sands ;
Gentle airs, like whispering voices,
    Come with meaning to his ear,
And his soul that hour rejoices,
    Knowing that his rest is near :
Slumbering ocean, smiling West—
All around him breathes of rest.

Grey upon the sunny slope
    Spreads the cross its stony arms ;
Rock of our unfailing hope,
    Blessed shield from mortal harms !

On the cross Columba leaning,
  Lustrous-eyed, with hoary hairs.
Meekly calm, unfolds the meaning
  Of the whispering spirit airs,—
Change to come ere dawn of morrow,
Joy to him—Iona's sorrow.

Brighter lustre fills his eye,
  Seer-like as he utters there
Words that, till remembrance die,
  Loving memories shall bear ;
Dear Iona's praise foretelling,
  Gazing round its shores the while—
"Widest, richest realms excelling,
  Thou shalt be, O blessed isle,
Loved and sought by kings and sages—
All the good through all the ages !"

Holy is the midnight time,
  Midnight in Columba's cell ;
Dearer than the sweetest chime
  Sounds to prayer the solemn bell.
Waking from his peaceful slumber,
  Rising from his couch of stone—
Cloistral darkness, age's cumber
  Heeds he not, but all alone

To the altar hastes aright,
Led by love's divinest light.

There he bends his aged knee,
    Sinking in the shadows dim;
There Iona's family,
    Grief-foreboding, seek for him.
Children of Columba's guiding,
    Brothers of one faith, are they,
In one rule of love abiding,
    Vowed to watch, to work, to pray,
Till the night of death shall fall,
Till their Lord his servants call.

"Father, where art thou?" they cry,
    With a thought of fear, a dread
Lest some brother's voice reply—
    "Weep, for he we loved is dead!"
Trembling hands with gleaming torches
    Soon the doubtful shadows end,
Pallid faces crowd the porches,
    Loved companions o'er him bend—
O'er Columba bend and weep,
Falling, in their arms, to sleep.

Silent are his lips and pale,
    Silent for all time he lies,

Yet, when words of blessing fail,
   He with wordless blessing dies ;
For his hand gives loving token,
   Slowly raised with dying breath ;
They, ere morning's dawn hath broken,
   O'er the very form of death
High are lifting, hopeful-hearted,
Praises for a saint departed !

II.

ST. MARGARET OF SCOTLAND.

THE historical line of the queens of Scotland has its glorious beginning with St. Margaret. The queen who preceded her, known to the curious by the name of Gruoch, and to all the world as " Lady Macbeth," belongs to poetic fable rather than to history. Margaret was grand-daughter of Edmund Ironside, an elder brother of Edward the Confessor, and was born in Hungary, whither her father Edward had been banished by King Canute. The Confessor recalled his exiled nephew with his family in 1057, and Margaret's early youth was passed at the English Court. About 1070, after the defeat of Harold's forces by William the Norman, she sailed from England with her brother Edgar Atheling, and her mother and younger sister, intending to return to Hungary, but tempestuous weather drove them towards the Scottish coast. With great difficulty their ship was brought into the Frith of Forth, and at length into a small bay, since called " St. Margaret's Hope," westward of North Queensferry, a name also commemorative of the Saxon princess. She was little more than twenty years of age, and of great beauty, with a winning gentleness of manner, which she ever retained, the faithful index in her of a soul endued with every christian grace. The tradition is, that King Malcolm Canmore, residing at the time in Dunfermline, a very few miles distant, and hearing of the arrival of the strangers, hastened to give them a personal welcome, and found Margaret, fatigued with walking from the ship, resting by the wayside, on what is still pointed out as "Queen Margaret's Stone." (Chambers's Picture of Scotland, 1840.) Their union soon followed, and never was a royal marriage happier in its results to the parties, or productive of greater benefit to their people. She effected a great reformation in manners and in religion, and all classes of the community regarded her with affection and veneration, most of all the king himself, who was wholly devoted to her, loving whatever she loved, adorning with costly ornaments, and frequently kissing, her books of devotion. During the conferences held by Queen Margaret with the clergy for the removal of various abuses that had crept into the church, he acted as interpreter, explaining to them her Saxon speech, and to her their Celtic. She introduced the observance of a liturgy more consistent with catholic usage than the corrupt forms then prevalent in Scotland. She

effectually prohibited Sunday labour.   Her alms-
giving, her fasting, and unwearied religious exercises,
are described in the affectionate biography written
by her confessor Turgot, a Benedictine monk, even-
tually bishop of St. Andrews, who dedicated the
work to her daughter Matilda, Queen of Henry I. of
England.—(Pinkerton's Vitæ Antiquæ Sanctorum.)
In November 1093, while she lay on her death-bed,
at Edinburgh Castle, her husband and two of her
sons were in Northumberland fighting against the
English.   On the 16th of the month one of them,
Edgar, arrived at the Castle, and told how the king
and her eldest son had fallen in battle.   On the
same day, shortly after hearing the intelligence, she
expired, holding in her hand the cross she loved—

" The dear remembrance of her dying Lord."

Her favourite cross was one of gold, about the
length of a palm, with an ebony figure of our
Saviour studded with gems, and a fragment of the
" true cross" enclosed in it.   This was the " Black
Rood " long preserved by the Scots, and sometimes
borne before their armies.   Malcolm and Margaret
were buried before the rood altar in the Abbey
Church of Dunfermline, the stately edifice erected
by the Queen herself on the spot of her happy

nuptials. Of their surviving children three sons
Edgar, Alexander, and David, became kings of
Scotland in succession, and gave evidence, the
youngest especially, that the teaching of their saintly
mother had sunk deep into their hearts. One well-
known incident connected with St. Margaret I must
add, not indeed for its own sake, but for the inference
drawn from it by our simple-hearted forefathers
entirely in accordance with her character while living.
On the accession of Alexander III. in 1253, he
desired that the remains of his great ancestress
should be removed into the choir, as a more honour-
able resting place. A great number of people
assembled, and a solemn service was performed with
chanting, and the music of the organ. It is related
by Andrew Wynton, the chronicler, that it was
found impossible to remove the coffin of the Queen,
until the body of King Malcolm also was lifted, for
the purpose of having the like honour paid to it.
Wynton, expressing the common feeling, says :—

> " This miracle to record,
> Notes great reverence to her lord,
> As she used in her life,
> When she was his spoused wife."

II.

St. Margaret of Scotland.

When Ninian from his holy toil
　　Had passed to rest with God,
And loved Iona's wave-worn soil
　　No more Columba trod;

When long long years of strife had paled
　　Devotion's heavenward flame,
Their prayers for Scotland still prevailed—
　　And Saxon Margaret came.

To Malcolm's court came Saxon lords,
　　From Hastings' fatal field,
With manly scars from Norman swords,
　　And wounded hearts unhealed;

Lamenting Harold's glory set
　　In blood at manhood's morn,
Lamenting high-born Margaret,
　　A fugitive forlorn.

The hope of Edward's royal race,
   And English hearts was she,
The maid who from the Norman's face
   Sought refuge o'er the sea.

But stormy blasts assailed her bark—
   The maiden feared no ill ;
The skies were tempest-torn and dark,
   Yet she was dreadless still.

When wildly roared the driving gale,
   She sang a holy psalm ;
The foam flew white o'er mast and sail,
   But all her soul was calm.

Ah ! not again to English land,
   Where ruled the Norman foes !
To bear her to the Scottish strand,
   The winds of God arose.

And ye, blest elder saints, with joy
   Saw her lone bark upheld,
Through surges powerless to destroy,
   Where Forth's broad water swelled !

Within Dunfermline's palace near,
　　The harp's high strain accords
With songs of welcome sung to cheer
　　The landless Saxon lords.

From princely daïs rise, Canmore,
　　A nobler guest to greet,
And bless the storm that to thy shore
　　Hath turned her wandering feet !

With kindly words her welcome speak,
　　In haste her bower prepare ;
The rain-drops chill her pallid cheek,
　　The rude wind lifts her hair.

And there that night, a welcome guest,
　　Reposed the Saxon maid ;
But ere to slumber's needful rest
　　Her weary limbs she laid,

The psalms of holy church she sung
　　Alone within her bower,
Extolling Him, with grateful tongue,
　　Who stayed the tempest's power.

And rose again her holy song,
    To Him at dawning prime,
Who guards his faithful ones from wrong,
    In all the storms of time.

God's service thus her sweetest food,
    She kept the perfect way,
The part of Christian maidenhood
    Fulfilling day by day ;

Till woman's meekness side by side
    With manly worth was seen ;
Till love enthroned her Malcolm's bride,
    And shouts proclaimed her queen.

And seated high in palace hall,
    Where chiefs and dames had place,
Her meekness crowned her, midst them all
    Of more than royal race.

O then the truths, her maiden years
    Had silently set forth,
She taught, with earnest speech, the peers
    Who ruled the rugged North !

c

She said—"The weekly Rest restore,
    To God and labour due ;
The half-forgotten round, once more,
    Of fasts and feasts renew :

" From pleasure fast, from stately pride,
    With alms and humble prayer ;
And ever in your feasts provide
    The friendless poor a share.

" For you, for them, in death's cold shroud
    The world's Redeemer lay,
And yours the shame, if want shall cloud
    Their joy on Easter day."

Blest Queen of Scots ! with richest store
    Of grace divinely fraught,
And wise in all the sacred lore
    By saints and martyrs taught ;

'Twas hers high mysteries to teach,
    In accents lowly sweet,
While priestly fathers listened each,
    As at an angel's feet.

True wife, whose gentle suasion led
　　Her husband's will to good !
Mother of kings, whose nurture fed
　　Their souls with heavenly food !

No holy maid, self-consecrate
　　To years of lonely prayer,
In cloistral peace her hour to wait,
　　Unvexed by worldly care,

Hath won so well the glorious meed
　　Of saintly name as she,
Who hallowed thus by word and deed
　　The state of royalty.

III.

THE INVASION OF HACO.

On the 2d of October 1263, Scotland was released from a danger which had for many months overhung its shores. Early in the year, the Scots had heard that their old enemy Haco, king of Norway, had, at the preceding feast of Christmas, summoned all the warriors of his kingdom to assemble under his banner in the spring, for the purpose of recovering possession of the Western Isles, and carrying dreadful vengeance among the peaceful subjects of Alexander III. On the anniversary of the day made sacred through all time by the heavenly tidings of "Peace on Earth," the Norwegian monarch sent forth his proclamation of war. The Scottish king, then in the 23d year of his age, was on his part determined to spare no means of defence against the invading Norsemen. All the principal castles in the country, from Ayr to Aberdeen, were strengthened, and all his subjects able to bear arms got them in readiness to resist the enemy at whatever point the attack should be made. It was, however, 'to the

Hebrides and the other islands near the western coast, that Alexander turned his most anxious attention. It had long been felt by his predecessors and himself, that the security and prosperity of the Scottish mainland absolutely required that the western sea should be freed from the piracies of the savage chiefs who pretended allegiance to Norway, an object to be accomplished only by securing to the Scottish crown the firm possession of those islands, and restoring that natural connection with them which the power of the Norsemen had severed. But the very independence of Scotland was now at stake. So well was Haco's summons answered, that in the beginning of July he was able to lead from the harbour of Herlover an armament more powerful and magnificent than any that had previously sailed from the Norwegian shore. In about two days his fleet arrived at Bredeyiar, or Brassay Sound, in Shetland, and by the 18th of July it was at Kirkwall. Meanwhile King Alexander had recourse to negotiations, which, if they failed, might delay the advance of the hostile fleet until autumn, when the uncertain weather incident to that season would, it was anticipated, embarrass its operations. When this result took place, and Haco, seeing his proudest vessels shattered by the tempest as they laboured on towards the Ayrshire coast in the ensuing September, imputed his disasters to the incantations of the Scottish witches, Alexander might have said, "this only is the witchcraft I have used." Under the belief that a darker agency was employed against him, Haco ordered the service of the mass to be chanted on one of the islands of the Cumbrays by the priests who accompanied him. At last the Norwegian fleet, despoiled by the storm of its original magnificence, yet presenting a most formidable appearance, was seen from the heights of Largs. The first resistance the Norsemen encountered as they leaped from their boats was from the weapons of the Scottish peasants, who had assembled in considerable numbers in defence of their native fields fearlessly opposing their untaught strength to the practised attack of those

> " Norwegian warriors grim,
> Savage of heart and large of limb."

Next day, the 2d of October, the Scottish knights spurred to the combat, led by their youthful king, who shewed himself brave in battle as he was wise in council. The issue of that day's long and bloody conflict impressed the hoary Norse leader—as with the feeble remains of his once numerous array of ships and warriors he returned to Orkney—with a deep sense of the over-ruling power of that Almighty One who had not gone forth with his host. Broken-hearted and repentant he laid himself down to die, declaring, says the old Chronicle of Melrose, "that he was repulsed not by the strength of man, but by the power of God, who had destroyed his ships, and sent death into his host." He was not permitted to see another Christmas day; for on the 15th of December, at midnight, the eyes of the aged warrior were closed in death.

III.

THE INVASION OF HACO.

HEAR how Heaven's protecting hand
    Aided Scotland's brave of yore,
Loving well their native land,
    Fighting for its sacred shore !

High in hope, from Norway's coast
    Haco steered his navy's pride ;
Shouted all his mighty host
    O'er Bredeyiar's swelling tide.

Gales of promise o'er his bark
    Shook the Raven banner's fold ;
Round the lofty prow so dark
    Angry dragons shone in gold.

Men and ships—hów great a band
    Through the Hebrid Isles hath gone !
Crested warriors crowded stand,
    Mail-clad rowers ply them on.

Who shall rashly, vainly, dare
Lead against him ship and sword?
Homage paying, quick repair
Mona's prince, and Isla's lord.

Who shall meet his vast array?
—Hark, the storm is answering!
Will the winds allegiance pay?
Will the tempest homage bring?

Wandering in the stormy gloom,
Darkling moved the ships, and slow;
And the lightning's dart of doom
Paled the golden dragons' glow.

Norway's wildered leader spake,—
" Muttering hags in Scottish caves
Thus the deadly tempest wake,
Rousing high the charmed waves.

" Priests, begin the rites divine,
Break with psalms the evil spell,
O'er the wildly surging brine
Let your voices loudly swell!"

Sadly in the storm they cried
   From the rocks in holy strain :
Feebly on the blast it died,
   Sadly, feebly, and in vain !

Still the tempest fiercer woke,
   Sweeping o'er each crowded deck ;
Still the billows, as they broke,
   Downward crushed some shrieking wreck,

Till the nearer shores of Clyde
   Saw the hostile navy sail,
Breasting o'er the foamy tide,
   Stoutly struggling with the gale.

Soon to land the Norsemen spring,
   Gathering fast, and gathering aye :
Alexander, Scotland's king,
   Meet at Largs the foe's array !

Warned by many a beacon red,
   Roused by many a battle horn,
Faithful-hearted, thither sped
   Stalworth Scots, from eve to morn.

Clad in mail from head to heel,
  Hasted thither knight and lord,
Yet the foremost foeman's steel
  Rattled on a peasant's sword.

Alexander, Scotland's king,
  Guarded well his sires' renown,
Willing warriors marshalling
  Seaward forth from dale and town.

Heard ye not their steeds by night
  Thundering by, as on they dashed?
Saw ye not at Largs how bright
  Sunrise on their armour flashed?

There the shout that warriors love
  Burst at morning's early glow;
Heaven's loud tempest raged above,
  Battle's storm was rife below.

Deeper grew at noon the fray,
  Murkier moved the troubled sun;
Sank in night his feeble ray
  Ere the bloody strife was done.

Glory to the Heavens on high,
    Combating for Scotland there !
Roaring wind, and sea and sky
    'Gainst the Norsemen fighting were.

Woe for Norway's sinking band !
    Darkness hid them, battle-worn,
Staying each contending hand,
    Darkness sweeter than the morn.

Woe for Norway's hapless king !
    Baffled hope oppressed him sore ;
Struck by sorrow's deadly sting,
    Back he turned from Albyn's shore.

Kingdom, kin, and native land
    Never, never shall he see ;
Borne from Orkney's fatal strand
    Dead and shrouded shall he be.

There, upon his dying place,
    Wounded in his soul he lay ;
There the spirits of his race
    Crowded round him, dim and grey.

Bid the pagan forms avaunt,
  By the charm of Christian prayer,
By the heavenward swelling chant,
  And the incense-perfumed air!

Answered then the warrior king,—
  "Priests, though sweetly in mine ear
Sounds the holy strain ye sing,
  Pagan spirits sadly hear.

" Yet awhile in rushing verse
  Let their daring deeds be told :
Bid the hoary bard rehearse
  Chronicled achievements old.

" Giant-hearted were my sires,
  Though but shadows now they seem :
Fiends of night through cavern fires
  Howling fled their falchion's gleam.

" Not from man or fiendish charm
  Come this bitter loss and woe ;
Higher, holier, mightier Arm
  Lays old Norway's honour low."

Thus at midnight's awful hour
　　Scotland's stern invader died :
Scotland's king, in princely power,
　　Sheathed his sword in battle tried.

Thus shall Heaven's protecting hand
　　Help the brave for evermore,
Loving well their native land,
　　Fighting for its sacred shore.

IV.

THE BIRTH OF THE BRUCE.

MARJORY, Countess of Carrick in her own right,
was married first to Sir Adam de Kilconquhar, and
afterwards to Robert de Bruce, son of that Robert
Bruce, Lord of Annandale and Cleveland, who was
subsequently competitor with John Baliol for the
Scottish crown. Her former husband was one of
the leaders of the force sent out on the part of
Scotland to join the Crusade set on foot by Louis
IX. in 1268, and was slain in Palestine. The
younger Bruce assumed the cross at the same
time, attaching himself to the companion force of
Prince Edward of England, afterwards Edward
I. Shortly after his return from Palestine, he met
with the widowed Countess, then in the pride of her
youth and beauty, and married her, under the circumstances described in the following ballad. It is
not improbable that his intimacy with the good
knight Sir Adam, had something to do with the
romantic affection which sprung up between her and
his surviving friend. She was a ward of the crown
during her widowhood, and the risk of their

marriage being opposed by the king, Alexander III.,
who was too careful of the interests of his kingdom
to consider it a matter of indifference who should
become master of such an important strength as
Turnberry Castle, led them to a secret union. A
fine of large amount was exacted by the crown for
the breach of the feudal law thus committed. Bruce
on his marriage became Earl of Carrick, which was
therefore one of the titles of his illustrious son,
Robert the First, born on 21st March 1274.

The childhood of the future deliverer of Scotland
was most likely spent at Turnberry, and this is
enough to make the present remains of the castle
interesting in a high degree. About five miles
north from the modern town of Girvan, situated at
the mouth of the river of that name, the ruins "may
be seen upon the points of a rocky promontory,
which there projects into the sea from a low sandy
desert of several miles in extent. Though Turnberry
is dreadfully dilapidated, and even considerably worn
by the sea and weather, the vestiges of a drawbridge,
several large vaults or caves, and the extent of rock
covered by the ruins, testify, in a very impressive
manner, the former vast strength and importance of
the fortress." (Chambers's Picture of Scotland.)

IV.

THE BIRTH OF THE BRUCE.

YE Scots whose faithful bosoms keep
    Old freedom's sacred flame
Unquenched and pure from age to age,
    From age to age the same ;

For you no fabling tale I sing,
    Bold hearts to Scotland true ;
Nor deadly battle's stormy theme,
    Free Scots, I sing for you.

Ye maidens, twine the blue-bell flowers,
    Around the thistle twine,
And hear a happy lay of love
    And liberty divine !

One summer noon, O brightest day !
    There chanced a knight to ride,
Pricking his steed in listless mood,
    By Girvan's woody side.

D

The lightly soaring lark, unseen,
  A heavenly carol sung,
And ceaseless warblings answered it
  The leafy boughs among.

Companionless the knight rode on
  Along the forest glade,
Content such music to enjoy,
  Such luxury of shade ;

For late on Syria's burning plains
  The trump of war had led
His sword where battle's din arose,
  And Moslem foemen fled.

As through the wood he went, he heard
  Some huntsman wind his horn,
And on the breeze the cheerful sound
  Of laughter lightly borne.

He listened, and sweet voices, clear
  As lark's at morning prime,
Sang merrily, and nearer came
  The hawkbell's tinkling chime.

And soon a bevy blithe advanced,
　The forest arches threading,
Their palfreys softly o'er the grass
　And ferny clusters treading.

The nimble huntsmen foremost ran,
　_The tangled boughs dividing,
And burst to sight a lady bright,
　With all her ladies riding.

Beneath her woodland cap and plume
　Her hair was darkly straying ;
Within her gentle eyes the light
　Of life's sweet summer playing.

The sunshine of a joyous heart
　Was in her smiling shewn;
And bore her brow no other gem
　Than purity alone.

Her face all beauty, beaming truth,
　The form her boddice bound,
Entranced his eyes, and o'er his heart
　An instant magic wound.

With courteous greeting, bending low,
  He reined his steed aside,
With seeming haste, and lingering glance,
  Along the glade to ride.

Outspake the dame of heart so free,—
  " Why haste you thus, Sir knight?
Fear not, though we be strong in force,
  And you in single plight.

" No Paynim Soldan's horde is here,
  Then safely ride with me,
For welcome to my lonely towers
  A wandering knight will be."

Again he bent him low in selle—
  " O dame beyond compare !
As through these forest paths I came,
  With wild blooms decked so fair,

" What form of fairy power, methought,
  The greenwood rules around?
And lo ! the queen of love appears,
  With beauty brightly crowned !

" But pardon, lady, if unstayed
    My journey must be sped,
Nor add unto the witching lure
    Already o'er me shed."

The lady and her maidens all
    ⌐The captive knight surround,
And powerless is the warrior's arm
    Whom gentle love hath bound.

.

Within her hand so soft and small
    She seized his bridle rein ;
And through the wood, with hawk and horn,
    In triumph rode the train.

They cleared the wood, they crossed the wold,
    Bright gleamed the waves of Clyde,
And Turnberry's stately walls and towers
    Looked o'er the ocean wide.

Within those walls, till even-song,
    A guest the knight remained,
And morning shone, and there was he
    In beauty's thrall detained.

He little recked the hours that fled,
    The days that went and came ;
He looked but to his lady's eyes,
    And they were still the same.

Twice seven days have come and gone,
    And morning's beams are breaking ;
The heavings of the deep afar
    Are in the sunlight waking.

Across the waves, along the shore,
    The silent dawn is stealing,
Those darkly spreading castle walls
    And shrouded towers revealing.

The lattice of the chapel dim
    Admits the holy beam,
And carven roof and pillared floor
    Are brightening in the gleam.

And there a priest white vestured stands
    To bless a kneeling pair :
'Tis he, the knight by love enthralled.
    And she, that lady fair !

That fairest dame is Countess high
Of Carrick's hill and vale ;
That loving knight is bold De Bruce,
Young Lord of Annandale.

The wedding words were spoken there,
—Unknown to kith or kin ;
And shall it please the Scottish king,
To dare his ward to win ?

But little cause her kindred found
The Border knight to spurn :
Nor long did Alexander's breast
With kingly anger burn.

Fair Marjory, what hopes swelled high
Thy loving heart to see
Thy bright-eyed first-born smiling sit
Upon his nurse's knee !

What dreams of manly graces stored
To charm the coming time,
The beauty of his rising youth,
The glories of his prime !

Yet even to thy thought could ne'er
Fond love that day reveal
When Bruce in all his manhood rose
To work his country's weal.

O ever blest from age to age
The woodland meeting be,
That gave a Bruce to Bannockburn,
And kept our Scotland free !

V.

THE WEDDING MASQUE OF ALEXANDER THE THIRD.

WORDSWORTH says of Presentiments :—

"When some great change gives boundless scope
To an exulting nation's hope,
Oft, startled and made wise
By your low-breathed interpretings,
The simply meek foretaste the springs
Of bitter contraries.

" Ye daunt the proud array of war,
Pervade the lonely ocean, far
As sail hath been unfurled;
For dancers in the festive hall
What ghastly partners hath your call
Fetched from the shadowy world !"

The incident of the skeleton masquer's sudden and startling appearance among the wedding revellers, which is the subject of the subjoined verses, occurred in Jedburgh, at the marriage of Alexander with Joleta, daughter of the French Count de Dreux, on the 5th of April 1285. "Her extreme beauty, the splendour of the suite of French nobility who accompanied her, and the generous wishes of the Scottish

nobles to manifest their joy at the marriage of the
king, and to efface all melancholy recollections from
his mind, rendered these festivities unusually
brilliant."—(Tytler's Scottish Worthies,—Life of
Alexander III.) Alexander had great cause for
melancholy. In the course of a few years he had
mourned the death of the queen, Margaret, whom he
espoused in his youth, of his two sons Alexander and
David, and of his only daughter Margaret, married
to Eric, king of Norway. His union with the
Princess Joleta renewed the hopes of his attached
subjects, that the royal line of Malcolm Canmore and
St. Margaret, in direct succession, would continue to
rule the North. Within twelve months after the
nuptial festivities at Jedburgh they experienced
bitter disappointment. The prediction said to have
been uttered by Thomas the Rhymer, that a terrible
storm would shortly burst over Scotland, was considered to be fulfilled by the sudden calamity which
befell the country in the loss of its king. On the
16th of March 1286, when he was riding in the
dusk of evening towards Kinghorn, along the cliffs
overhanging the Frith of Forth, his horse stumbled,
and fell with him down a precipice, causing instant
death. The next stroke of evil suffered by the Scots
was the death of the last of Alexander's family, his

grand-daughter Margaret, the "maiden of Norway," whom, during his lifetime, with the deepest anxiety for the future, he had solemnly bound the states of his realm to recognize as their rightful sovereign, and who now, while only in her eighth year, leaving her father's caresses to dwell with people she had never seen, was attacked by disease on her way to Scotland, and died in Orkney. But these events were merely the beginning of sorrows. They were soon followed by all the miseries which a contested throne, the usurped and tyrannical rule of a stranger, and the traitorous submission of their chiefs, can bring upon a free people.

King Alexander's daughter was attended on her way to Norway by several of the Scottish nobility, who perished by shipwreck on their return ; a circumstance which would be afterwards noted by the people among those warnings of future calamity that crowded·the latter years of Alexander's reign. To this event the ballad of " Sir Patrick Spens" is supposed to refer.——(See Additional Notes at the end of the volume, for some remarks regarding the ballad just mentioned.)

V.

THE WEDDING MASQUE OF ALEXANDER THE THIRD.

HOPE evermore foreruns the birth
    Of joy in hearts most drear,
And mourning never follows mirth
    But with a boding fear,

A prophesying of the heart,
    A dimming of the eye,
The sounding of a coming dart,
    A shadow stealing by.

And oft rejoicing nations know
    More palpable and sure,
More dread betokenings, that foreshow
    Their joy shall not endure.

Dull minstrel hence! a blither lay
    In festive hall be sung!
King Alexander weds to-day
    A princess fair and young.

And Scottish maidens in the dance,
　　To tabor, lute and song,
Move with the laughing lords of France
　　In mirthful maze along.

The harpers, harping in the hall,
　　Their monarch's praises swell ;
From famous chieftains, warriors all,
　　His high descent they tell.

And all, in love and homage there,
　　Look gladly on the king,
While flowers before his lady fair
　　The bridal maidens fling.

Some sit entranced at beauty's feet,
　　Around the banquet some,
When hark ! with music wild and sweet,
　　The merry masquers come.

Like elves that eldern forests haunt,
　　They troop in quaintest guise ;
How light their steps, how jubilant
　　And bright their glancing eyes !

" The elfin king, the elfin queen "—
   To pipe and harp they sung,
Tripping beneath the branches green
   Within the palace hung :

" The king and queen of elfin land
   Rule o'er the forests free ;
The wild deer own their sceptre wand,
   And we their lieges be.

" Their home the giant thistle wards,
   Their couch is thistle down,
And aye the faithful Lion guards
   The elfin realm and crown.

" And long o'er happy elfin land
   Shall last their peaceful reign ;"—
Why shuddering part the mirthful band ?
   What dumbness stops their strain ?

As if some old and hidden grave,
   Beneath the masquers' tread,
There to the light untimely gave
   Its shroudless, fleshless dead,

Upstarted in the midst a form
  That rattled bone on bone,
Long while deserted by the worm,
  And left in dust, alone.

In festive hall, a moment's space,
  It mocked with dismal glee
The masquers' lightly changing pace,
  Alone and silently ;

And ceasing soon its cheerless play,
  Sudden, with outstretched arm
And pointed finger, passed away;—
  Heaven shield the king from harm !

The sun rose brightly on the morn,
  And hearts, that yesternight
With boding fear had sunk forlorn,
  Beat high with new delight.

That form was not of charnel birth !
  'Twas but a painted show,
A cunning pageant meant for mirth,
  Portending weal nor woe !

But hoary heads that shook with age
    Hoarded the token still,
Devoutly waiting, sad and sage,
    The surely boded ill.

And Ercildoune's unerring seer,
    Who sat by Eildon tree,
Foretold some mighty tempest near,
    Some woe that yet should be.

O deadly was the storm that came,
    And bitter was the woe,
The weird of misery and shame,
    The Scots were doomed to know !

The monarch of their heart to mourn
    Lying in gory plight,
Down from the cliffs of steep Kinghorn
    Cast in the wildering night :

An infant from a distant land
    Their rightful queen to own ;
Full soon to know that Orkney's strand
    Had heard her dying moan.

And, woe of woes ! dark tyranny
  Spread forth its dragon wing ;
And liberty waxed faint to see
  Its death-like shadowing.

Truth languished in the dust o'erthrown,
  As treachery grew strong ;
And noble hearts became as stone,
  Through misery and wrong ;

Till right had over countless foes
  A glorious victory won ;
Till liberty exulting rose,
  And Scotland's weird was done.

VI.

BALIOL THE PAGEANT KING.

THE "mournful melody" introduced into the accompanying ballad is preserved by Wynton as a song of lament made after the death of Alexander III.—

> "Quhen Alysandyr oure kyng wes dede,
>   That Scotland led in luive and le,*
>   Away wes sons† of ale and brede,
>   Of wyne and wax, of gamyn and gle ;
>   Our gold wes changyd into lede.
>   Cryst, borne into virgynyte,
>   Succour Scotland, and remede,
>   That stad is in perplexyte."

The character of Alexander was in every respect worthy of the affection which his subjects entertained for his person and memory, while the peace and prosperity which distinguished his reign made the subsequent condition of the Scots the more intolerable.   Wynton himself says :—

> "Scotland menyd him full sare,
>   For under him all his lieges were
>   In honour, quiet, and in peace ;
>   Forthi called Peaceable King he wes."

---

* Tranquillity.   † Abundance.

After the successes of Robert I. had restored to
the country a great part of its former happiness and
tranquillity, the days of the earlier monarch were
long remembered as "the time of peace ;" and until
a change took place very recently in the ancient
forms of the Scottish Chancery, relative to the
service of heirs, the reign of Alexander was referred
to in the—same terms, when mention was made of
the old valuation of the lands " *in tempore pacis.*"
The ancient lyric inserted above may, it has been
conjectured, refer in part to the discontinuance of
the liberal supplies granted to the monasteries by
King Alexander during his lifetime. " Bread, wine,
and wax" (as in the instance mentioned in connection with the " Battle of Bannockburn," *infra*),
were articles often presented to religious houses and
churches, and the thoughts of the unknown minstrel,
probably an ecclesiastic, very naturally recurred to
the abundance of such gifts in past years, when he
sought to describe the melancholy change that had
taken place in his native land.   His verses, however,
breathe a higher spirit, and express a national
sorrow.

The dishonourable reign of John Baliol commenced in 1292, and terminated, by his deprivation,
in 1296.

VI.

BALIOL THE PAGEANT KING.

The trumpets blared through Stirling town,
  In measured breathings sounding long,
As trooped in gorgeous pageant down,
  From Stirling towers, a marshalled throng.

Champed the proud steeds, their trappings gay
  With high heraldic blazon glowed,
And, chiefest of the plumed array
  Of Scotland's peers, De Baliol rode.

Though kingly was the pomp, and clear
  The heralds' music swelling high,
Yet Baliol ever longed to hear
  His people's living voice reply.

But feeble were the shouts as passed,
  Like a dark cloud, the vain parade,
That dimmed the eye of age, and cast
  On tearless manhood's brow a shade.

They could not hail with joyful look
  The nobles who had wronged their land,
Or shout before a king who took
  His kingship from a stranger's hand.

There, 'mid the crowd of lowly born,
  One nameless Scot stood by to see ;
The meanest page had passed in scorn
  A lowly Frere so poor as he.

Yet, not unknown among the brave,
  An iron coat and blade he bore,
When Alexander's freemen drave
  King Haco from the Scottish shore.

And now within his aged eye
  For the old glory rose a tear ;
For high-born shame he heaved a sigh
  And burned in thought, that lowly Frere.

" O where is he, and where are they,
  The leader and the band so true,
Whose worth shall wipe our shame away,
  And Scotland's golden years renew !

" Where free hearts beat, where round the hearth
   The ready swords are hung, I know ;
But Scotland's chiefs forget their birth,
   And John to Edward bends him low.

" Ah, Baliol, Baliol, thou hast won
   A bitter portion, hard to bear !
Confessed as king supreme by none,
   Yet suffering all a kingdom's care.

" Thy lordship was enough for thee ;
   Less worship now thine honours bring,
And thou hast learned how poor must be
   A sceptred thrall, a subject king."

Thus, sad in soul, the aged Frere
   By winding Forth pursued his way,
Until he heard a maiden near
   Sing to her task a simple lay ;

A mournful melody that plained
   For Alexander, fated king !
How loved, how royally he reigned,
   And left his people sorrowing :—

" When Alexander our king was dead,
    That Scotland led in love and le,
Away was sons of ale and bread,
    Of wine and wax, of game and glee ;

" Our gold was changéd into lead ;
    Christ, born into Virginity,
Succour Scotland, and remedid,
    That stad is in perplexity !"

Warm in his heart such blitheness sprung,
    As there his feeble steps he stayed,
Kind Heaven he blessed, and her who sung,
    For he that simple song had made.

Proudly he held his way alone,
    And while that strain was in his ear,
King Edward on the English throne
    Was poorer than the lowly Frere.

VII.

THE PENANCE OF JOHN BALIOL.

ON St. Andrew's day, 1292, John Baliol was enthroned as king of Scotland, after swearing fealty to Edward I., whose commissioner placed the crown upon his head. The coronation took place at Scone, and it was the last time that the Fatal Stone was used for such a purpose within the limits of Scotland. The crime of thus surrendering the liberties of his country received its merited punishment. The yoke of the Lord Paramount was soon found insupportable by Baliol and his peers, and at last King Edward's peremptory summons to attend him in his campaign against Philip of France drove the Scottish barons to renounce, in Baliol's name, all allegiance to the English monarch, a step which they followed up by an invasion of his kingdom. This, however, tended only to exasperate Edward. Determined to crush what he deemed a presumptuous rebellion, he entered Scotland with a powerful army, captured and pillaged the rich town of Berwick, and totally routed the Scottish forces at Dunbar. The ceremony with which the reign of

Baliol terminated, on the 7th of July 1296, was
scarcely more degrading than that which inaugurated
it. His feudal penance, as a rebellious vassal, was
performed in the churchyard of Stracathro, in
Angus, before Anthony Beck, bishop of Durham, as
Edward's representative ; and the remembrance of
the event still lingers, it is said, in the tradition of
the district. The presence of the great English
peers, with their men-at-arms, and the position
occupied by the warlike prelate, who was himself
commonly attended by a hundred and forty knights,
must have made the ceremony as imposing as the
appearance there of the wretched vassal-king was
full of shame. On the 10th of July his formal
resignation of the kingdom into Edward's hands
took place at the castle of Brechin.

A few months afterwards Sir William Wallace
began his ever memorable career.

VII.

THE PENANCE OF JOHN BALIOL.

" Come rest thee, Father, here awhile,
    For thou art travel-worn ;
Bless a poor widow's roof to-night,
    And speed thy way at morn.

" My youngest son the heather sweet
    Will pull, thy bed to be ;
My eldest from the broomy burn
    Will bring a fish for thee."

" All blessing, daughter, evermore
    With thee and thine remain !
And they that succour wandering age
    A full reward shall gain.

" My limbs are old and weak, kind dame,
    My wandering steps are slow ;
But sorrow is a heavier ill,
    And sad in heart I go.

" Mine eyes are old and dim, in sooth,
　　But better had they been
　Beneath December's snow-drift closed,
　　Ere they that sight had seen,—

" That sight of never dying shame
　　 —I saw but yester morn ;
　A Scottish king in penance stand,
　　And brook the Southron's scorn !"

" Good father, he was worthy scorn,
　　Such craven soul to shew !
　But say, how happed the deed of dole
　　That fills thy heart with woe ?"

" Not thus it sank with sorrow, dame,
　　When Edward, in his pride,
　Bade our Scots lords in England's host
　　With John his vassal ride,

" And manfully in wrath they spurned
　　His summons and his power,
　Renouncing for their king the faith
　　He pledged in evil hour.

" They rode from east, they rode from west,
   But rode and strove in vain ;
For resteth not with mortal might
   The victory to gain.

" Fore-doomed the conflict's issue lies
   In Heaven's own counsels deep,
But honour, though a world be lost,
   A man, unarmed, may keep.

" The English king to Brechin tower
   Passed on in conquering state,
Where Baliol, stricken in his pride,
   Stood singly at the gate,

" A suppliant for lands and life,
   A beggar for the grace
Of one that, as a rebel seri,
   Now spurned him from his face.

" And at Stracathro, by the kirk,
   Before this July sun,
Where many a Scot sleeps low in death,
   Was Baliol's penance done.

" I saw proud Durham's bishop there,
  In purple weeds arrayed,
On cloth of gold sit royally
  Beneath the elm trees' shade.

" The English barons, dark in mail,
  Stood by, a noble ring !
Each like the leader of a host,
  And stately as a king.

" And there, in presence, pale King John,
  With sceptre, robe, and crown,
Bent on the kirkyard's trampled sod
  His vassal eyes adown.

" Most like a pageant king he looked,
  A pageant king was he,
Losing no kingdom when he lost
  His robe of royalty.

" They lifted from his head the crown
  That Alexander wore,
And from his grasp the sceptre took
  That Alexander bore.

"The rod of penitence instead
   His trembling hand displayed,
While to the Southron priest his lips
   Their hoarse confession made,

"Of foulest treason to his lord
   In striving to be free,—
All, but his first foul treason done
   To Scotland's liberty!

"And could I there forget the time—
   A patient, soulless slave—
When never foeman's heel durst spurn
   The humblest Scottish grave?

"Could I but weep? The Southron loons
   They mocked me for my tears,
And thrust me on my joyless path
   Away before their spears.

"And now I wander wearily,
   With mournful thoughts opprest,
Beside my childhood's home at last
   My aged bones to rest.

" But they, methinks, shall stir with life
   In the grim charnel gloom,
When banded freemen first shall march
   In triumph past my tomb !"

VIII.

WALLACE OF ELDERSLIE.

To introduce the next piece, I need mention only
that the first exploit of this disinterested champion
of liberty was achieved in 1297.   Early in 1298
he was elected Governor of Scotland, in name of
John Baliol, who was still recognized by the Scots as
sovereign of the country, notwithstanding his forced
resignation.

VIII.

WALLACE OF ELDERSLIE.

'Tis not alone with present years
—The free-born patriot's spirit dwells,
Nor only with their hopes and fears
    His bosom sinks or swells.

He loves to turn him to the morn
    Of liberty, and proudly mark
Its dawn upon a land forlorn,
    And desolate and dark.

He loves to watch, he claims to share,
    The never failing hopes that cheered
The struggling brave all toils to bear,
    And death itself endeared.

Then turn, ye patriot Scots, with me,
    To Scotland's time of thrall, and sigh
For banners fallen with the free,
    Who freely dared to die.

F

Her ramparts and her halls behold,
   How scorched around, and lone within,
Or shamed with banners strange, and sold
   Through treason's deadly sin !

Invasion's burning breath has charred
   The greenness of her spring, and wide
Her summer fields o'er-sweeping, marred
   The hope of harvest tide.

And rust is on the sickle's blade,
   The household quern's blithe whirl is dumb,
From sunny lea and grassy glade
   No herds at evening come.

Despair the wasted lowland fills,
   Oppression loads the lowland air,
But hope is wafted from the hills,
   For liberty is there !

The Southron heard, when night was near,
   The wild wolf's cry come down the glen,
And, shuddering at a sound so drear,
   His wassail sought again.

The Scot knew well that signal sound,
    And, arming with a freeman's pride,
He hasted to the gathering ground,
    Along the mountain side.

And one by one, as stars grew bright,
    They came, who loved their native land ;
Beneath the pine-wood's double night
    They stood, a daring band.

But forth at midnight flashed the dawn,
    The stormy dawn of liberty,
When at thy word their swords were drawn,
    Wallace of Elderslie !

Wallace of Elderslie ! my lay
    Would linger with thy name, and wake
Fondly and wisely, that it may
    Be loved but for thy sake.

Wallace of Scotland, her true knight,
    True peer of a dishonoured throne,
When Scotland's king betrayed his right,
    And cared not for his own !

Prince of the faithful who have wrought,
    Not for themselves, but to obtain
Their country's good, and purely sought
    To rescue, not to reign !

Doth not the Scot who can retrace,
    Through changing years of sun and gloom,
To thee the freedom of his race,
    Revisit oft thy tomb ?

Ah where ?   There is no grave for him
    In all the land he loved, no field
Of battle where his eye grew dim,
    And death his witness sealed.

To the four winds his limbs disperse !
    So doomed the vengeance of his foe ;
Yet shall not thence the poet's verse
    Be but a dirge of woe.

Though hearts that loved him then were riven,
    His deathless spirit moved them still,
And, wider than his bones were driven,
    It breathed on moor and hill.

His spirit conquered at the last ;
　His name was marvellous in might ;
And Scotland, when her toils were past,
　Remembered Wallace wight.

IX.

THE JUDGMENT OF WALLACE.

SIR WILLIAM WALLACE, until his betrayal in 1305, had continued to defy the armies of the English king, and with a company of brave men, few but faithful, awaited in the forests and mountain strongholds of his native Scotland the hour that might again place him in a situation to restore her to freedom and peace. After the Knight of Elderslie was delivered to the English, and carried to London, he was brought to Westminster Hall, where he was made to sit on a low bench; "a crown of laurel was placed in mockery upon his head, as it was reported he had been heard to boast that he deserved to wear a crown in that place; and Sir Peter Mallorie, the king's justice, rising from his seat, impeached him as a traitor to his sovereign, the king of England; as having burnt the villages and abbeys, stormed the castles, and slain the liege subjects, of his master. 'To Edward,' said Wallace, ' I cannot be a traitor, for I owe him no allegiance ; he is not my sovereign ; he never received my homage ; and whilst life is in this persecuted body he never shall receive it. As to the other points whereof I am accused, I freely confess them all. As governor of my country, I have been an enemy to its enemies. I have slain the English; 1 have mortally opposed the English king; I have stormed and taken the towns and castles which he unjustly claimed as his own. If I, or my soldiers, have plundered or done injury to the houses, or to the ministers, of religion, I repent me of my sin, but it is not of Edward of England that I shall ask pardon.' Upon this confession, he was immediately found guilty, and condemned to death. The sentence was carried into execution on the 23d of August, with every circumstance of refinement in cruelty. Having been dragged upon a hurdle, with his hands chained behind his back, to the foot of a high gallows, erected at the Elms in Smithfield, he was placed on the scaffold, surrounded by all the dismal apparatus of torture. At this awful moment he preserved an unshaken serenity. He requested the attendance of a priest to whom he might confess himself, and it is painful to learn that Edward, who was present, in a fit of obstinate and impotent resentment, denied him this last comfort. Winchelsea, Archbishop of Canterbury, however, who stood near the scaffold, boldly reproved the king for interfering, with his temporal authority, in a matter exclusively religious.

'The Church,' said the faithful prelate, 'will not
suffer any of her penitent children, whatsoever may
have been his guilt, or to whatever country or
kindred he may belong, to request the offices of a
priest in his last moments and to be refused, and I
myself will officiate, since none other is so near.'
Saying this, he ascended the scaffold, received the
confession, and gave him absolution, after which he
departed for Westminster, unwilling to be a spectator
of the cruelties which were to follow. At this
moment Wallace entreated Lord Clifford, who stood
hard by, that a psalter, which had been taken from
his person, should be restored, and the request was
complied with.   As his hands were chained, he
desired a priest who was near him to hold it open ;
and it was observed that, during the whole time, he
regarded the volume with a look of mingled devotion
and affection.—This psalter had been his constant
companion from his early years."—(Tytler's Scottish
Worthies.) The head of Wallace was placed on
London Bridge ; and his right arm was sent to
Newcastle, the left to Berwick, his right leg to
Perth, and the left to Aberdeen ; "to be gazed
upon," says the English Chronicler Langtoft, "instead of the gonfanons and banners which his
abettors had once so proudly displayed."

IX.

THE JUDGMENT OF WALLACE.

HIGH in the hall of doom
King Edward's liegeman see !
Death's darkest shadow palls with gloom
    The solemn pageantry.
Ah, woeful pomp ! Ah, gloomy day
That reft a nation's hope away !

The traitor, where is he ?
    Behold, with laurel crowned,
A form of strength and majesty,
    In felon fetters bound !
Unworthy fetters ! can there lie
Base treason in that kingly eye ?

'Tis Wallace, 'tis the Scot !
    Can aught of felon shame
Dishonour with a darkening blot
    The ever glorious name
Of him whom grateful thousands mourn,—
Their Wallace from his country torn ?

Say, hath he pledged his truth
　　King Edward's faith to follow,
Yet, spite of honour, void of ruth,
　　With faithless heart and hollow,
Hath traitor been, and in the land
Destroyed and slain with rebel hand?

Say, hath ambition fell
　　Swayed his all-daring sword ?
No ; but he loved his country well,
　　And tyranny abhorred !
In this his deadly treason lies ;
For this by tyrant power he dies.

They mock the Scot in vain
　　With crown of laurel there ;
He strove no monarch's crown to gain,
　　Nor wealth nor power to share ;
Yet more than kingly name and might
Exalts the praise of Wallace wight.

He was the first who called
　　Aloud for liberty,
Teaching a people, sore enthralled,
　　To will and to be free ;
His dearest, loftiest wish to stand
The guardian of his native land.

When Scotland's glad acclaim,
From foes awhile released,
Was hushed, and Scots of noble name
The strife ignobly ceased,
Amid his native mountains he
Wandered a houseless man, but free.

Delivered to his foes
When yet his arm was strong,
And in the ear of hope arose
His rescued country's song,
He stands, no traitor, but betrayed,
Death-doomed though 'twere an angel prayed.

Proud king ! thy thirsting sword
Won thee a victor's fame,
Yet what hast thou, usurping lord,
Of Scottish hearts to claim,
That they thine island birth should prize,
Or triumph for thy victories ?

But lasting as the hills,
And as the valleys dear,
Wide-spreading as the countless rills
That hill and valley cheer,
The memory and name shall be
Of him who died to set them free !

X.

KING ROBERT THE BRUCE.

THE flight of Bruce from the English court, which Scotland may consider as, in some measure, the Hejira of her independence, took place in February 1305-6, at a time when the Scottish patriots were few in number and despairing in heart, for never had the prospect of success against the power of Edward I. appeared so distant. The popular tradition of the circumstances attending the event is thus given by Lord Hailes :—"The king, having drunk freely one evening, informed some of the lords about his person that he had resolved next day to put Bruce to death. The Earl of Gloucester hearing this resolution sent a message to Bruce, with twelve-pence and a pair of spurs, as if he meant to restore what he had borrowed. Bruce understood that this message warned him of his danger, and counselled him to flee. Much snow had fallen during that night. Bruce ordered a farrier to invert the shoes of his horses, lest he should be traced in the snow, and immediately set out for Scotland, accompanied by his secretary and his groom."—(Annals of Scotland, vol. I., p. 320 ; but see Appendix in vol.

III.) Robert I. was crowned at Scone by Wishart, Bishop of Glasgow, on the 27th of March 1306; and again formally installed, or, as some writers express it, a second time crowned, on the 29th of the same month, by Isabella, Countess of Buchan, and sister of the Earl of Fife ; she having suddenly arrived among the brave men there assembled, and claimed the honour of placing the sovereign on the throne, as a right belonging to her brother's family from the days of Malcolm Canmore. Both her husband and brother were then in the English interest. For this act she was subsequently punished by the English monarch, who caused her to be imprisoned in a cage latticed with wood, cross-barred and secured with iron, constructed in an outer turret of Berwick Castle ; and she continued thus barbarously confined for a period of four years, till removed to a monastery.

"The Bishop of Glasgow," says Mr. Tytler, "supplied from his own wardrobe the robes in which Robert appeared at his coronation ; and a slight coronet of gold, probably borrowed by the abbot of Scone from some of the saints or kings who adorned his abbey, was employed instead of the hereditary crown," carried away by King Edward—(History of Scotland). If the coronet had been obtained in the manner conjectured, somewhat fancifully, by the historian, the abbot would likely have taken care to replace it when the ceremony was over. We know that it shortly afterwards fell into the hands of Geoffrey de Coigners, for there is extant a pardon, granted on 20th March 1307, to a person of that name by King Edward, at the suit of his Queen, Margaret, "for the offence of retaining and concealing the coronet of gold (coronella aurea) with which Robert de Bruce, now in rebellion against us, lately caused himself to be crowned in our province of Scotland." (Rymer's Fœdera).

One of the chapters of Hector Boece's History (Bellenden's Translation) bears the title,—"Of King Robert Bruce's Coronation, and of his great miserie." These few words, expressing ideas which we do not commonly associate together, have a touching simplicity about them, and illustrate very fitly the historical truth. The "miserie" followed hard upon the "coronation." We are told by Barbour that, when, about three months after that event, the small army of patriots was surprised and defeated at Methven by superior numbers of the enemy, the "new made king" (as an English knight scornfully styled him) and the few who remained to share his fortunes,

"As outlaws went mony a day,
Dreeing in the Mount their pyne."

They wandered long among the mountains which
stretch between the Tay and the Dee, eating only
what they procured by hunting, and drinking the
water that rilled from the corrie ; without shoes but
what they made with their own hands from the skins
of deer ; and unable to communicate with the low
country for needful supplies, because obliged to dis-
trust all that were not of their own company. It is
true there were along with them the Queen and
other ladies,

"That for leal love and loyalty
Would partners of their pains be ;"

but they felt these privations the more keenly that
they were endured by those who were far less able
to bear them. Long the outlawed king wandered,
with a still smaller band, amidst the wilds of Galloway and of Lorn, with blood-hounds on his track,
the swords of his own countrymen turned against
him on every side, and too often receiving intelligence
of some dear relative or friend put to death, or held
in miserable captivity, on his account ; his wife and
daughter torn from sanctuary and carried away to
prison in England. But may it not be said, what
was probably felt by the noble-hearted Bruce himself,

that this was a punishment inflicted on him for a
deadly though unpremeditated crime—the murder
of the Red Comyn in the Greyfriars' Church at
Dumfries, immediately after his flight from England?
A portion of that honest hatred which attaches to
Macbeth and the Crook-back Richard might have
fallen on King Robert, if any lasting success had
immediately followed the sacrilegious slaughter of
his powerful rival.   It was doubtless good for him
that he had to endure a trial of eight weary years
between his coronation and the victory at Bannockburn.   That victory was indeed his crowning glory,
but it is the patient resolution with which he sus-
tained the severest reverses and sufferings in the
intervening period, that has made his career so
deeply interesting, his manly character so exalted,
and his achievements to receive, in every age, the
glad sympathy of all who love their country.

X.

KING ROBERT THE BRUCE.

High offspring of princes, and kinsman of kings,
To thee the lorn hope of the desolate clings ;
For Scotland lies wasted, and spoiled is her throne ;
The Bruce to the rescue,—to rescue thine own !
From thraldom the land of thy fathers deliver ;
   The home of thy mother is longing for thee ;
O haste ere our hope shall have perished for ever
   With him, the lost warrior of lone Elderslie !

The gay Southron halls and their harping forsake,
And the songs of the North in thine honour shall wake,
Nor the days of thy strength in the tourney beguile,
The bright lance of freedom all shivered the while.
O bide not the guest of our country's enslaver,
   Whose walls her lost banners in trophy display !
Unblest is his friendship, deceitful his favour,
   His minions are watching thy words to betray.

But speed thy swift courser to fair Annandale,
Where loyalty's welcome thy coming shall hail ;
Each shout by Tweed river far echoed shall be

From the mist-shrouded wilds of the Don and the Dee.
Though stern be the conflict, and perils assail thee
    Long watching and toiling in forest and field,
True hearts shall be near thee, strong hands shall
    not fail thee,
    And right be thy panoply, Heaven be thy shield.

When Lennox and Athole thy summons shall hear,
With Hay and with Douglas their bands will appear;
And the knights of thy blood every danger will dare
For a brother they love, and the name that they
    bear.
Then come o'er the Border, the lustre restoring
    Whose splendour encircled the old Scottish throne
Till years of glad triumph for days of deploring,
    And Bruce for the shame of a Baliol atone !

The Bruce o'er the Border came riding with speed,
Oppressors defying by word and by deed,
And 'midst of his foemen, in moorland and glen,
The banner of liberty lifted again.
O fearless as fair was the lady who crowned him,
    And royal the circlet she claimed to bestow ;
And brave were the barons who shouted around him,
    "Heaven prosper King Robert, and tyrants o'er-
    throw !"

XI.

THE BATTLE OF BANNOCKBURN.

THIS battle was fought on the 24th of June 1314. Besides the Scottish king, the principal leaders of the patriot army were his brother Edward Bruce, his nephew Randolph Earl of Moray, Sir James Douglas, and Walter the High Steward. At this moment Scotland enjoys important advantages resulting from the victory then obtained over the host of Edward II. One remarkable circumstance attending the battle is, that it was fought, as it were, by appointment, and the very field of engagement almost marked out a year previously. This was in consequence of King Robert's unwary brother, while prosecuting the siege of Stirling Castle, in June 1313, having agreed to the treaty proposed by the English governor, Philip de Moubray, that he should surrender the fortress if not relieved before the Feast of St. John the Baptist, the 24th of June, in the ensuing year. The King, though greatly disapproving of such an arrangement, was of too chivalrous a disposition to think of acting contrary to the agreement made by his brother. Both sides, accordingly, had twelve months to prepare for the final struggle. The result was that England brought to the field at least 100,000 men, and Scotland about 30,000 ; the available forces of the latter country being summoned from all quarters. It may be conceived how anxiously the whole Scottish people must have looked forward to the inevitable day of meeting, and, as the appointed time drew near, how eagerly the inhabitants of the distant northern towns must have sought for tidings from the south, making them ready to exalt the slightest incident into something of importance. A story which Hector Boece tells is an illustration of this. "On the same day that this battle was stricken, a knight with shining armour showed to the people at Aberdeen how the Scots had gotten a glorious victory of Englishmen. Soon after, he went over Pentland Firth ; and was holden by the people to be Saint Magnus, prince sometime of Orkney ; and for that cause King Robert dotat (endowed) the kirk of Orkney with v. lib. sterling of the customs of Aberdeen, to furnish bread, wine, and wax, to the said kirk." St. Magnus was Earl of Orkney from 1103 to 1110. In the accounts rendered by the Bailies of Aberdeen to the royal Chamberlain, there are repeated entries of a payment of £5, the precise

sum specified above, received yearly by the Bishop
of Orkney, in virtue of a Gift by King Robert I.—
(Chamberlain Rolls, vol. I. p. 487, under date 1368 ;
and vol. II. p. 153, under date 1390.) The charge
appears to have been faithfully defrayed by the
burgh till the end of the 16th century.—(Spalding
Club Miscellany, V. pp. 111 and 372.) The payment is the more remarkable that the Bishop of
Orkney was not a Scottish prelate at the date of the
earlier entries referred to ; the territories forming his
diocese not having been annexed to this country
until 1468, although the bishops were not unfre-
quently Scots by birth. A strong presumption is
thus raised that the king did actually execute such a
grant as is mentioned in the story quoted, and not
improbably with express reference to the reported
apparition of the martyred earl. I am not aware
that the document is now extant.

The standard of Bruce was planted on the Bore
or Bored Stone, still remaining an object of veneration to Scottish pilgrims ; and when Queen Victoria,
during her progress in Scotland in 1842, passed
along the field of Bannockburn, it was a right
feeling that caused the UNION FLAG to wave from
the same spot.

LINES WRITTEN AT THE BORE-STONE, IN SEPTEMBER 1839.

FIVE hundred years ago, here stood
  The banner of a marshalled host ;
And here, five hundred years ago,
  A field was won and lost.

What then ? Full many a bannered sign
  Hath waved defiance to the foe,
And many a field been lost and won,
  Five hundred years ago.

But let no Scot unmoved declare,
  No friend of freedom coldly learn,
That banner was the Bruce's sign,
  That field was Bannockburn !

XI.

THE BATTLE OF BANNOCKBURN.

FOR Scotland and the Bruce,
    A cry to battle filled
The weary land, and to the Isles
    The far-borne summons thrilled :
From Cheviot to the Pentland sea,
    Ye who the dread of dying spurn,
For liberty, for liberty,
    Advance to Bannockburn !

There must a fight be fought,
    There must a field be won,
Ere Freedom from the conflict rest,
    In deadly strait begun.
Hark ! from the glens and forests free
    The gathering Scots that cry return !
For liberty, for liberty,
    We meet at Bannockburn !

My heart is with the chiefs
    Who marshalled there on field,
In bannered lines, an iron host,
    With pike, and blade, and shield ;—

King Robert, in himself a band,
   Lord Edward, ever fierce in fight,
Bold Randolph of the lightning hand,
   And Douglas, dreaded knight.

They saw no blenching cheek,
   No wandering eye, disclose
The failing of one Scottish heart,
   Though trebly ranked their foes ;
Though England's king his armies spread,
   Crowding the burdened plain afar,
And peers a hundred singly led
   A thousand men to war.

And when, on battle's eve,
   The Scottish trump on high
Bade all unsworn that fight to win,
   Or with their king to die,
To quit unharmed that fated wold,
   How proudly burst one shout in air,
That by its mighty concord told
   No voice was wanting there !

Along the lines at morn,
   On lowly knee they fall ;

But not to thee, vain English king,
  With craven look they call !
From Heaven's eternal armoury
  For strength in battle's hour they prayed,
Then high of heart, unbent in knee,
  The shock of battle stayed.

They stayed and stood the shock ;
  Though death-bolts dimmed the sky,
None in that hour his faith forgot,
  None faltered but to die.
And still as charged the baffled foe,
  Like stormy billows raging wide,
The Scots' firm front, without a blow,
  Rolled back the roaring tide.

Now, Scotland, for thy cause !
  Bends, breaks the English line :
For liberty, for liberty
  Shout, for the charge is thine !
And well did Scotland's burning host
  Charge home upon that glorious day,
When crushed was England's tyrant boast,
  And fled her king away.

The death her thousands died,
  The fears of those that flee,

Were as the righteous pangs that racked
    Expiring tyranny.
And Scotland shall remember long,
    Nor English hearts the conflict mourn,
For Freedom sang her triumph song
    That day at Bannockburn.

XII.

THE DOUGLAS' PILGRIMAGE.

THE Romances of Chivalry afford no narrative more
beautiful than that which history gives of the friendship of Bruce and Douglas. King Robert died at
Cardross, upon the Clyde, on the 7th of June 1329,
of a disease originating in the privations he had
suffered in his wanderings. As Barbour expresses
it,—

> "Through his cald lying,
> When in his great mischief was he,
> Him fell that hard perplexity."

The feeblest language can never deprive of interest
the scene of his last parting with the Good Sir
James, who had so well aided him in the great
strife for freedom, never swerving from his loyal
obedience since the day when he hastened to salute
the uncrowned Earl as his sovereign, and who now,
with equal readiness, though with many tears, promised on the faith of a knight to fulfil the Bruce's
last command—to carry his heart to the Holy
Sepulchre. In September 1329, the young king
Edward III. granted a passport to Douglas, on his

journey "to the Holy Land, in aid of the Christians
against the Saracens, with the heart of Robert, king
of Scotland."—(Rymer's Fœdera). In the same
collection, there is also a letter from Edward to
Alphonso XI., king of Castile and Leon, of the same
date as the passport, recommending Sir James to
his royal favour.   It may be hence inferred that the
Scottish knight entertained from the first the design
of assisting the Castilian king ; and he was no
doubt prepared, if need were, to fight his way to
the walls of Jerusalem.   The graphic narratives of
Barbour and Froissart have made familiar the inci-
dents of the journey which Douglas thus undertook,
and which was terminated, on the 25th of August
1330, by his death in the battle of Theba, in Anda-
lusia, fought between king Alphonso and the Moors
under Osmyn, commander in Granada.   On the death
of Sir James Douglas, the knights who had crossed
the sea in his company appear to have considered
it unnecessary to proceed further on an expedition
for which he alone had been specially designated,
and they therefore brought back the heart with
them to Scotland.   In depositing the precious relic
with the monks of Melrose, however, they complied
with the request contained in a letter addressed by
King Robert " to David, his beloved son," on the

11th of May 1329, about a month before his death, commending to his particular care the interests of that monastery, " in which, according to our special and devout injunctions, our heart is to be buried." (Chartulary of Melrose, as quoted in Tytler's Scottish Worthies.) The monastery had suffered very severely in the War of Independence, and had been in a great measure restored by King Robert from the state of ruin in which the inroads of the English had left it.

Barbour gives Douglas a place in his poem almost equal to that occupied by the hero whose name it bears, and has left us an interesting description of his personal appearance and demeanour, often quoted :—

> " In visage he was some deal grey,
> And had black hair as I heard say ;
> But of limbs he was weill made,
> With banes great and shoulders braid.
> His body was weill made and lenye,
> As they that saw him said to me.
> When he was blithe he was lovely,
> And meek and sweet in company ;
> But quha in battle might him see,
> All other countenance had he.
> And in speech lispet he some deal,
> But that sat him right wonder weill."

Another passage in the same poem shews that

Douglas' manner of fighting on the field of Theba during the whole engagement corresponded with the act which immediately preceded the last onslaught he made.

> " The Bruce's heart that on his breast
> Was hanging, on the field he kest
> Upon a stone-cast, and weill more,
> And said, ' Now pass thou forth before,
> As thou was wont in field to be,
> And I shall follow, or else die.'
> And so he did, withouten ho.
> He faught even till he came it to,
> And took it up in great dainty ;
> And ever in field thus used he."

Nearly five hundred years after the great King Robert had been laid in his marble tomb, before the high altar of the Abbey Church of Dunfermline, in the sight of all the prelates and nobles of the kingdom, and a vast concourse of his people, it happened, on the 17th of February 1818, that his remains were revealed for a while to the eyes of their descendants. The discovery was made in clearing the foundations for a new building on the same site, and as soon as circumstances permitted, the bones of the Bruce were reverently interred of new. The identification of the body was complete. The breast bone was found to have been sawn asunder that the heart might be removed. Around the skull the lead which encased the remains had been twisted into the form of a jagged crown. And well may the Scots whose fathers he delivered, and who themselves experience the happy effects of the Good King Robert's toil and victory, as they now stand beside his tomb, remember with gratitude his travail, and say,

Requiescat in pace !

XII.

THE DOUGLAS' PILGRIMAGE.

THE good King Robert dying spake,
  His barons wept around ;—
" Friends of the Bruce ! to Death I yield,
  But there is Ransom found !

" And laud be to the Power that kept
  My life from manhood's prime,
And to a blood-stained soul vouchsafed
  A blest repenting time !

" Sir James of Douglas, brother dear,
  True friend in weal and woe !
Thy name and mine, companions still,
  To other times shall go.

" Recall that summer noon we lay,
  Beneath the sultry sky,
In wild Glengairn, whose waters yet
  I hear go rushing by ;

"How there with tales of bold emprize
    We sped the dreamy time,
  Writ in the olden history,
    Or sung in minstrel rhyme ;

"Of knightly feats, and spurs well won,
    In fight with Paynim powers,
At Acre's shore, or Ascalon,
    And Zion's leaguered towers.

"'Twas then a solemn vow I breathed,
    When Scotland peace had seen
In tower and hamlet, glen and isle,
    And foes had banished been,

"My way to far Jerusalem
    With fitting heart to wend,
A pilgrim, and a warrior, there
    My sinful days to end.

"Jerusalem ! my steps would fail
    To thy dear Mount to fare ;
This dying hand is now too weak
    A pilgrim's staff to bear ;

II

" But ever fondly longs my heart
 Within thy courts to be,
For all the blest and glorious things
 Declared and done in thee.

" Douglas ! be thine the trust to bear,
 When Bruce is lying low,
This heart to far Jerusalem,
 In sight of friend and foe."

The Douglas to the dying Bruce
 Listened as one forlorn ;—
" My liege beloved, that trust I'll take,
 Or live a knight forsworn !"

Tombed in Dunfermline's sacred choir
 King Robert lowly lay :
The good Sir James with honour passed
 On pilgrimage away.

Within a silver casquet shrined
 The heart of Bruce he bore,
And ever, as a friend beloved,
 Near his own heart he wore ;

While like a crowned king he held
  His journey o'er the sea,
With noble knights, and squires to serve,
  Nor squires of low degree.

The good ship to the Flemish strand
  With kindly breezes sped :
" Here tarry we, dear friends, a space."
  The loving Douglas said.

" For here, upon the ocean free,
  The Bruce his court shall hold,
And welcome give, as he was wont,
  To all true hearts and bold."

The bugles sounded to the shore,
  Forth streamed the banners fair,
That friend and foe might soothly know
  A king of Scots was there.

Brave knights there came from Flemish land,
  Brothers in arms to be :
" Friend of the Bruce, lead on," they cried.
  " 'T is fame to follow thee !"

And all who to the Douglas' board
  Came greeting, prince and page,
Cried, " Honour to the kingly Heart
  That goes on pilgrimage!"

But tidings were to Douglas borne
  That, fired with frantic zeal,
Granada's chief in arms defied
  The knights of fair Castile.

Out spake the pilgrim knight,—" Be ours
  To drive from Christian ground,
Back to their scorched and desert homes,
  The hordes of false Mahound!

" For craven is the pilgrim's heart,
  That buckled steel would shun ;
Nor wont was I the deed to fly,
  King Robert's self had done.

" Unmoor the ship!"   The ship unmoored
  Sped proudly o'er the main,
Till knights and squires and spearmen trod
  The martial fields of Spain.

They heard the Christian clarions wind
　　Their notes to warriors' tread ;
They heard the Moorish trumpets bray
　　Their larums deep and dread.

They saw the red-cross banners brave
　　In sunny splendour stream,
— And 'midst the turbaned Moslem foes
　　The baleful crescent gleam.

It was the hour ere fight hath joined,
　　Or signal trumpet blown,
When breathlessly the cavalier
　　Reins in his champing roan ;

When prayers are muttered, vows ascend,
　　Adieus are briefly paid,
Ere swords be shattered, plumes be shorn,
　　And warriors lowly laid.

Proud was the Christian king to greet
　　A knight so good and brave,
And as a king to crowned king,
　　The welcome that he gave,

In honour of the noble deeds
  That swelled the Douglas' fame,
In honour of the noble Heart
  That with the Douglas came.

"I yield thee here, Sir James," he said,
  "The vanguard line to lead :
The Arm that aided Bruce and thee
  This day thy prowess speed !"

Then joined the eager hosts, and roared
  The battle's wild affray,
Till broken fled, discomfited,
  The infidel array.

Now joy to Leon and Castile !
  The crescent gleams no more ;
And honour to the Scottish knights,
  But wail to Scotland's shore !

Wail for the hour when bold Saint Clair
  In mortal peril fell,
And Douglas spurred his steed to save
  The friend he loved so well !

Far from the Christian host he rode,
   Till rallying foes around,
And vengeful swords, the Douglas held
   Within their deadly bound.

But ceaselessly his blade he plied
   Among the Moslem crew,
And "Douglas to the rescue!" still
   He shouted as he slew.

King Robert's heart in casquet shrined,
   That by his corselet hung,
Stained with his streaming blood, he took
   And, rising, forward flung,

As rose his last bold cry above
   The battle's rout and roar,—
"Lead on, as thou wert wont, good Heart ;
   I follow, as of yore !"

And to the death he followed him,
   His liege and brother dear ;
Ah ! never had such noble king
   Such brave and loving peer !

And when in weeping quest the Scots
　　Passed o'er that battle ground,
Keeping his knightly trust in death
　　The good Sir James they found.

But not within the stranger's land
　　The Douglas' grave was made ;
In Douglas kirk his relics dear
　　By kindred hands were laid.

Nor yet to far Jerusalem
　　They bore the Pilgrim Heart,
For who so worthy as might claim
　　To do the Douglas' part ?

To Scotland's mourning strand again
　　Returning o'er the deep,
They gave the Heart to Melrose monks
　　In loving charge to keep.

Their eyes are dust who welcomed it
　　With gushing, grateful tears,
And watched its shrine by day and night
　　Through many troublous years.

The walls that gave it holy rest
 Are mouldering to their fall ;
The world's old faith from change and chill
 Hath suffered more than all ;

But noble spirits still delight
 To hear the story told,
_How Douglas bore in pilgrimage
 The heart of Bruce the bold.

XIII.

AGNES OF DUNBAR.

THE ancient castle of Dunbar, so important in the wars between the two kingdoms from its strength and situation, being the key to Scotland on the south-east, belonged to the Earls of March and Dunbar; and in 1337, during the reign of David II. the fortress was besieged by the English invading army under Montague, Earl of Salisbury, a leader of experience. The owner, Earl Cospatrick, was then absent, but his Countess, the daughter of Thomas Randolph, and grand-niece of Robert Bruce, with a spirit worthy of such descent, defended the castle, and for a long time resisted all the attempts of the enemy, who at last tried to reduce the place by famine. " Black Agnes" (as she was popularly styled), after a defence of five months, was fortunately relieved by the skill and intrepidity of Alexander Ramsay of Dalhousie, a knight well known in Scottish history, who, with forty men, aided by the darkness of night, passed from the Bass Rock, in a ship laden with provisions, to the besieged fortress, and, obtaining an entrance, continued the defence so

vigorously, that the English commander abandoned
the enterprise in despair. The bravery of the
Countess communicated itself to her female attendants, and Salisbury, while the siege lasted, had to
endure their repeated taunts. When a stone struck
the battlements, one of her maidens, by her direction,
would deliberately wipe the spot with a white napkin
in the sight of the enemy (a token of defiance
similar to that given by Sir Thomas Maule when
defending Brechin Castle against Edward I.), at the
same time that she returned a more effective answer
to their warlike missiles. " My lady's love-shafts go
straight to the heart !" cried the Earl, as an arrow
from the castle pierced the mailed breast of an
English knight beside him. The soldiers retreated
from Dunbar sorely annoyed by the sense of failure
under such circumstances, but loud in their praises
of the Dark Lady's courage and untiring efforts to
resist all attacks ; and a rhyme that sprung up
among them (preserved by Wynton), declares :—

> " Came I early, came I late,
>   I found Annot at the gate."

Her deliverer Sir Alexander Ramsay, for the
achievements he performed in behalf of his country,
in its harassing contest with Edward III., and for
the generosity of his character, better deserved to be

known as the "Flower of Chivalry," than the treacherous Sir William Douglas, the knight of Liddesdale, who was so styled, and by whose cruel violence he was brought to a miserable end. Coming upon the unsuspecting Ramsay at a moment when he had no means of resisting an attack, Douglas carried off his old companion in arms, and threw him into a dungeon of Hermitage Castle, where he was left to perish with hunger; a crime adding greatly to the load of infamy which, in the popular belief, had been weighing down the massive walls of the castle since the time when the last Lord Soulis held his unholy meetings there with the spirits of evil.

XIII.

AGNES OF DUNBAR.

No more of love's caressing !
  With longing looks and sighs
Let others woo the blessing
  That lurks in ladies' eyes :
I heed not love's alluring call,
  When freedom bids to war,
And foes surround thy castle wall,
  Dark Agnes of Dunbar !

Great Randolph's fearless daughter,
  Lord March's dame is she ;
Beside the ocean water
  Her towers embattled be ;
And Salisbury's Earl, from sea and plain,
  For five long moons hath tried
By might, by sleight, those towers to gain,
  That still his host defied.

The darkness of her beauty,
 Her proud eye's queenly glance,
Command a nobler duty
 Than song or wreathed dance.
They lead where danger lies before,
 And meeds that knightly are ;
To fight for Scotland's leaguered shore,
 And Agnes of Dunbar.

No longer idly lingers
 Her hand on harp or lute ;
Nor weave her snowy fingers
 Their golden fancies mute ;
For, waving from the rampart high,
 They mock the baffled foe,
Or bid the bowman's arrow fly
 To strike some leader low.

If feeble and unaided
 Her faithful band should yield,
With deep dishonour shaded
 Were Ramsay's name in field.
Then forth my men ! The sun hath set,
 And night hath not a star ;
In spite of odds, we'll succour yet
 Brave Agnes of Dunbar !

So Ramsay spake, unfearing,
   Dalhousie's peerless knight,
And through the darkness steering
   His laden ship aright,
Within the gate his troop at morn
   Were shouting, fresh for war,
And Salisbury won but scathe and scorn
   From Agnes of Dunbar.

XIV.

THE BURNING OF ELGIN MINSTER.

THE Cathedral of Moray, at Elgin, had stood for upwards of a hundred and sixty years, when, upon St. Botulph's day, 17th June 1390, it was destroyed by Alexander Stewart, Earl of Buchan, a son of Robert II., and from his many deeds of savage violence, well known in his own time and to posterity as the "Wolf of Badenoch." The destruction of the Minster was the last of a series of great crimes committed by him within a short period, and resembling more the acts of a demoniac than those of a sane person. Having been excommunicated by the Bishop of Moray, for keeping violent possession of church lands in Badenoch, he sought revenge by burning the town of Forres, with the choir of the church of St. Lawrence, and the house of the Archdeacon, in the end of May 1390. With scarcely any interval in his career of sacrilege and devastation, he attacked Elgin in the following month, and burned the town, the church of St. Giles, the Hospital or Maison Dieu, eighteen stately manses of the canons and chaplains, and, as already mentioned, "what was more bitterly to be deplored, the magnificent and beautiful Cathedral of Moray, the mirror of the land and glory of the kingdom, with all the books, papers, and other precious things stored up within it."—(Registrum Episcopatus Moraviensis.) In the same record appears a letter addressed by the bishop from Scone Abbey to Robert III., on 2d December 1391, in which the writer represents himself as weak through old age, ruined by repeated depredations and robberies, and so impoverished as to be scarcely able to procure for himself and his scanty household the necessaries of life, and complains that at the king's coronation he had, without avail, besought the royal aid in rebuilding the cathedral, which had been the ornament and delight of his native country, and the theme of praise with strangers and in foreign lands, for the loftiness of its towers, the richness of its furniture and innumerable jewels, and the multitude of its servants employed in fitly celebrating the worship of God ; that he had personally laboured with his canons for its restoration, till constrained to abandon his efforts for want of means ; and he therefore commends the cause of God and his church to the king, praying that the incendiaries might be brought to punishment and compelled to

make amends for the ruin they had caused. The
Earl of Buchan was at last obliged, for these crimes,
to undergo public penance in the Blackfriars'
Church at Perth, when he was absolved by the
Bishop of St. Andrews, acting by special commission
from the aged northern prelate. The rebuilding of
the cathedral was soon commenced, but owing to
the greatness of the work, and the unsettled state of
the country, many years were required to complete it,
although the bishop and his two immediate successors
in the see, with the clergy of the diocese, liberally
contributed their means. Ultimately, at a meeting
of the chapter, on 18th May 1414, the canons,
before proceeding to elect a new bishop, took an
oath that whosoever of their number should be
chosen would annually apply one-third of the
episcopal revenue towards the work of restoration,
till it were finished. The minster, when completed,
had five towers, two at each end, and one in the
centre, with a steeple reaching to the height of
198 feet. It would occupy too much space here to
recount the glories of the magnificent fabric as it
stood at the middle of the 16th century. It were
needless to describe what it is now.

XIV.

THE BURNING OF ELGIN MINSTER.

In Moray's glorious minster
     The faith of bygone days
Maintained the beauteous order
     Of sacrifice and praise ;
The faith of simple hearts that sought
     For fitting ways to give
All wealth to God who giveth all,
     And by whose breath we live.

The towers were fair and stately,
     And broad each sculptured wall ;
Rich light streamed o'er the altar,
     The fairest place of all ;
And day by day a chosen band
     Stood there, with skilled accord,
In chanted psalms and swelling hymns
     To magnify the Lord.

The goodly gate at dawning
     Was ever opened wide,

To win from care the lowly,
　　The noble from their pride ;
And oft the distant chimes at eve
　　The way-worn pilgrim cheered ;
Their sound to many a weary heart
　　By thoughts of Rest endeared.

Fallen Spirit ! foe undying
　　Of all things fair and good !
When pale with anger's madness
　　The Lord of Badenoch stood,
To God's true bishop dooming woe,
　　Woe to that stately pile,—
Dark tempter ! 'twas thy breath that stirred
　　His heart, his words the while.

Weep for the pride of Moray,
　　The glory of the land !
For Elgin's ruined minster,
　　Fired by the spoiler's brand.
Mourn with the lowly poor whose tears
　　Bedew the blackened sod,
Leaving their burning homes to weep
　　Around the house of God !

When died beyond the mountains
　　The clamour of the foes,

Within the roofless chancel
  The deep-toned chant arose :
" O Lord of mercy, Lord of love,
  On Thee our care we cast :
Be Thou our shelter till the storm
  Of man's fierce wrath be past !

"Lord, in thy love and pity,
  Look down from Heaven and see
The branch thy hand hath planted
  Of truth's eternal tree,—
How wasted by the ravening foe,
  Devoured by fiery flame !
O let its beauty rise again
  In glory to thy name !"

But other strains were chanted,
  High strains of hope and joy,
When he who led his vassals
  To ravage and destroy,
Had sought for peace with man and Heaven
  By penance and by prayer,
And Elgin's minster rose again
  From ruin, twice as fair.

For all the faithful-hearted
  Their offerings gladly brought ;

And skilled in works of beauty
    Were they who bravely wrought.
With mystic banners from the south,
    The craftsmen crossed the Spey,
And Elgin's priests with blessings came
    To greet them on the way.

The workers, the restorers!
    With more than craftsmen's pride,
They reared a lofty minster
    All change of time to bide.
They thought not that a time would come,
    A change from love to hate,
When Scots should be content to leave
    Its altar desolate.

XV.

YOUNG ROTHESAY.

The year 1401 is marked by the treacherous murder
of David, Duke of Rothesay, the eldest son of Robert
III., at the instance of his ambitious uncle the Duke
of Albany, and through the falsehood of his pretended friend Sir John de Ramorgny. Rothesay,
who was about twenty-three years of age, possessed
great beauty of person, was accomplished in literature,
and skilled in music, but fond of pleasure to excess.
He had previously been appointed, for a term of
three years, lieutenant or regent for his infirm father
over the kingdom, and had bravely defended the
Castle of Edinburgh, when besieged by Henry IV.
of England. The youthful prince had a weary time
to repent of his excesses, when he was so cruelly
left in the dungeon of Falkland Castle to perish with
hunger and thirst. " It is said that for a while the
wretched prisoner was preserved in a remarkable
manner by the kindness of a poor woman, who,
in passing through the garden of Falkland, and
attracted by his groans to the grated window of his

dungeon, which was level with the ground, became acquainted with his story. It was her custom to steal thither at night, and bring him food by dropping small cakes through the grating, whilst her own milk, conducted through a pipe to his mouth, was the only way he could be supplied with drink."—(Tytler's History.) But on these visits of charity being at length discovered by the ruffians who were appointed to await the death of their prisoner, she was made to pay for her loyalty with her life. The particulars as to the secret aid afforded to the prince are elsewhere stated thus :—" There is a tradition in Falkland that he was for a long time supported by two women, the wives of tradesmen in the town, one of whom purveyed bread to him through a chink in the wall of his dungeon, while the other conveyed the milk of her breast to his mouth by means of an oaten reed."—(Chambers's Picture of Scotland.) The present building forms part of the palace erected by James V., and the murder of Rothesay took place in an older castle which stood on the same site.

XV.

Young Rothesay.

Come where the greensward daisies rise,
    Dear lady of the western clime !
And clustering flowers whose glorious dyes
    And balms enrich our summer time ;

Come where old Falkland's palace walls
    Casting their evening shadows stand ;
And list the while my lay recalls
    A story of thy fathers' land !

There was a king in Scotland reigned
    Once in the fierce and lawless time,
When lands were won and power maintained
    By banded force or whispered crime :

Feeble of heart, in strength decayed,
    By vexing wiles and strifes undone,
The ruler of the land he made
    His first-born prince, his darling son.

Young Rothesay in his father's hall
   Had grown a bright and peerless flower,
But oft the boding tear would fall
   For him within his mother's bower.

In youthful fire and princely grace
   He moved, and gladdened all who saw ;
And needs not, lady, words should trace
   The form thy fancy best can draw.

Brave as a kingdom's heir should be,
   And whirled in pleasure's wild career,
Yet pure and gentle poesy,
   And music's voice, to him were dear.

Sweet minstrelsy he cherished well,
   And strains that, by their simple art,
Have made thy tender bosom swell,
   Had rule o'er Rothesay's wayward heart.

Praised for his bounty evermore,
   The favour of the land he stole,
But hatred for the love it bore
   Burned in one gloomy kinsman's soul.

And watched dark Albany the hour,
With serpent fang, and eagle eye,
When treachery and lawless power
Should bring his brother's child to die.

Dark was the hour, and black the night,
When Rothesay, by his friend betrayed,
Was torn from all his life's delight,
And low in Falkland's dungeon laid.

But, blacker than the midnight storm,
Despair's thick horror came in gloom,
When wasting hunger's ghastly form
Glared on his soul and marked his doom ;

When hours were added still to hours,
And day was joined to weary day,
And, unsustained, strong manhood's powers
Were sinking like his hope away ;

For none from fount or plenished board
Came to his need at morn or night ;
Yet Rothesay's sire was king and lord,
And he was next in royal right.

Still would his dreams, too quickly flown,
    The scenes of festive joy recall,
But waking famine saw alone
    The grim unchanging dungeon wall.

He thirsted for the dew that filled
    The blue-bell cups his lattice by,
And for the rain at eve distilled,
    That mocked his burning agony ;

Praying the fitful breeze of spring
    Through the close prison bars to bear
One drop of all 't was lavishing
    Against each thankless buttress there.

Alone he died ; but ere the night
    Of death upon his eyelids fell,
When hope was dark, the heavenly light
    Of woman's pity cheered his cell.

For she is ever kind and true,
    And night by night her secret care,
Her hand and voice, awhile withdrew
    Young Rothesay from his lone despair.

When other help was none, she gave
    Rich drops from life's sweet fountain drawn,
Through all the midnight's terrors brave,
    And trembling at the light of dawn !

But cruel eyes beheld her weep,
    ('Twas in the fierce, the lawless time),
Nŏr long could gentle woman keep
    Her prince from death, her land from crime.

And Rothesay's hope grew dark again,
    Though morning lit his dungeon floor,
For, done to death by cruel men,
    That lowly mother came no more.

Yet many a lay I'd sing to thee,
    Till day forsook our Scottish strand,
How woman's truth and loyalty
    Are honoured in thy fathers' land.

XVI.

THE BURGHERS OF BON-ACCORD.

In the words of the old rhyme :—

> " July twenty-fourth, St. James's Even,
> Harlaw was fought, fourteen hundred and eleven."

This battle was occasioned by the inroad of Donald, Lord of the Isles, upon the Northern Lowlands, arising from a dispute between that chief and Robert, Duke of Albany, Regent of Scotland, concerning the succession to the Earldom of Ross. The Islesmen, on coming to Harlaw, near Inverury, and about eighteen miles north-west of Aberdeen, were opposed by an army very much inferior to their own in numbers, commanded by Alexander Stewart, Earl of Mar, who had hastily gathered to his standard the barons and gentlemen of Aberdeenshire, Angus, and the Mearns. The burgesses of Aberdeen (well known by its ancient motto of "Bon-accord") were led out by Robert Davidson, the "Alderman" or Provost for the time, and greatly distinguished themselves in the bloody engagement which ensued. The result of the conflict saved not only the town of

Aberdeen, but a great part of Scotland from the
evils which the conquest of a civilized territory by
savage katerans would certainly have occasioned.
The Lord of the Isles used no greater threats than
he might easily have fulfilled, but for the determined
resistance thus made to the design he expressed, of
plundering Aberdeen and over-running the country
to the banks of the Tay. In the battle Provost
Davidson was slain, along with a number of his
fellow-citizens. His body was brought to Aberdeen,
and interred within the parish church of St.
Nicholas. It is characteristic of an age when the
sword was wielded more readily than the pen, to
find in the contemporary municipal record no
mention of the battle which had deprived the community of the chief magistrate whom they had
chosen at the preceding Michaelmas. That record,
however, contains a list of burgesses who were
"chosen to go out against the katerans." It is
found in the 1st volume of the Council Register,
(MS.) p. 291, among many entries connected with
the period of Davidson's aldermanship), and has
the appearance of being hastily written out upon
what had been a page previously left blank, and
originally intended for a more peaceful entry. There
seems good reason for assigning to it a date cor-

responding to the conflict at Harlaw, and it is too interesting to be omitted here.

" Electi ad transeundum contra Kethranos.

Simon Lamb.	Will : Gilruth.
Duncanus Hervy.	Thomas Chekar.
Thomas Henrici.	Joh : Roule.
Thomas Trayle.	Jacobus Lask.
Galfridus Taillour.	Thomas Roule.
W. Jacsoun.	W. Turyn.
Thomas de Tulch.	Gib. Meignes.
Adam cum Andrea Gilberti.	David Galrygyn.
Fynlaus Johannis.	Joh : Tulach.
Willelmus Johannis.	Duthacus Lownan.
Joh : pro Thoma Moden.	Joh : Yule, cum homine.
Walterus Bowar.	Andreas Guthry.
Joh : Moden.	Fynlaus Montagw.
Henricus Lethe.	Joh : Pypar.
Henricus Stephani.	Joh : Atkynsoun.
Nicholaus Plummar	Alex^r. Benyn, cum homine.

Simon Benyn, cum homine."

A few other names appear in the list, but have had the pen drawn through them ; a circumstance significant, perhaps, of the haste with which the magistrates had to provide means for opposing the advance of the enemy.*   It is probable that some

* These names are—" Joh. Crusank, Henricus Celey, Joh. Halk, Andreas Giffard, Will. Andree, et homo dicti ballivi,

others not named joined the chosen band. The Provost, in particular, would as a matter of duty take the post of leader. Francis Douglas mentions a tradition in his time "that the town made an act that in future their Provost should upon no occasion, whether of war or ceremony, go beyond the gates," (Description of the East Coast, 1782), and in this statement he has been followed by Sir Walter Scott (Hist. of Scotland); but it is remarked by a later author that "no trace of this regulation is to be found in the city records, and it may be therefore fairly set aside as apocryphal."—(Book of Bon-accord, by Mr. Joseph Robertson.) The story, indeed, is scarcely credible, but it may be mentioned that there is a blank in the record from 1414 to 1433. Aberdeen was never a properly fortified town, though, when occasion required, defensive works were no doubt thrown up at the points most exposed to attack.

A further notice of Robert Davidson will be found at the end.—(See Additional Notes).

Fynlaus cum Thoma Amfray, Joh. Rede, taillour." The leaves of the Register, at this early part, have been bound up in a confused manner.

K

XVI.

THE BURGHERS OF BON-ACCORD.

Sons of the busy lowland shore,
    Where bounteous Don and purest Dee,
Far from their native mountains, pour
    Their waters in the surging sea ;
Ye whom old honour's pride inspires,
Hear how, in days long past, your sires
    Free swords at need could draw,
All for their loves and household fires,
    And died at red Harlaw !

Sworn on the dirk to burn and slay,
    And ruthless as the wasting flame
That followed fast their murderous way,
    The host of fierce Macdonald came :
The clansmen of the western sea,
Who held the Isles in sovereignty ;
    They came, with hope elate
That all the Lowlands' spoil might be
    The harvest of their hate.

Lord of the Garioch's slopes and streams,
　Rose Benachie's dark frowning head ;
Dark, though the morning's brightest beams
　O'er the green summer woods were shed ;
Dark-frowning, for a redder glare
Widely to northward flushed the air,
　No kindling blaze of day ;
The fire that maketh waste was there,
　The spoilers and their prey !

And on through Foudland's cheerless glen
　Down on the Garioch burst the foe ;
By Ury's stream, ten thousand men,
　They rested on their course of woe.
Speed, knights of Angus, spur and speed !
Bowmen of Mar, advance at need !
　Burghers of Bon-accord !
Will ye your dearest ones should bleed
　Beneath the Islesmen's sword ?

At morn the 'larum bell rang out,
　With hurried beat went forth the drum,
From street to street there ran a shout,—
　" Arm ! To the cross ! The katerans come !"
Ah, then the burgher's look of care
Changed to a warrior's glance and air ;
　Then youth's first arms were clasped,

And he that erst did harness bear
His old blade fondly grasped.

Hark ! the burly bell is tolling,
    Louder still and louder rung,
From you tower its summons rolling,
    Clanging with a warning tongue.
Burghers, sworn and faithful all,
Well ye know its 'larum call ;
Guard the gates and man the wall,
    Watch and ward !
Silken weed for mirthful mumming,
    Painted bow for sportive sward,
Arms of proof when foes are coming ;
    Haste in harness, watch and ward !

Burghers, brothers, speed your arming,
    Coat of fence and blade prepare !
So the sudden foe's alarming
    Ne'er shall take you unaware.
Daily, nightly ready found,
Sentinel the city round,
Let the sleepless trumpet sound,
    Watch and ward !
Fight ! nor fear, in combat mortal,
    None be left your homes to guard :

Round each loved and lonely portal
Angels still shall watch and ward!

They banded fast, and band so good
Ne'er joined a haughty baron's fray :
For hearth and home they freely stood,
No thralled serfs, or hirelings they!
And he, their chief, no lordly load
Of titles bore, yet proudly rode
The Provost on his selle,
And baron-like his bosom glowed
To hear the trumpet swell.

High swelled the trumpet as they went
Forth by the gate, unfolded slow
And slower closing, for it sent
Dear hearts to meet a ruthless foe.
And they were gone, to bleed, to die,
And loving watchers wearily
Sighed the long sun away,
Watching in hope some dear one's eye
Might see him set as they.

The bell rang out at dead of night,
When the far winding of a horn
Came faintly, with the growing light
Of streaming torches townward borne.

O wasted still, or fled the Gael?
Returned the band with joy or wail?
   That lonely bugle sent
A changing note that breathed a tale
   Of triumph and lament.

'Twas the same band, returning all,
   The living and the dead, for there
The frequent corses to the wall
   Their wounded comrades feebly bare ;
And there, unvizored, pale and dead,
Stretched on his steed, where torches shed
   A dim and fitful ray,
The Provost came, and o'er him spread
   The town's broad banner lay.

That troop its dinted staff around
   From noon to night were seen to bide,
In press of battle foremost found,
   Striking for home, by Ury's side.
And Benachie at dawning day
Rose bright, when through the glens away
   Returned the baffled foe,
And Lowland homes, from Don to Tay,
   Were saved from wasting woe.

Sons of the North ! long years have known
   Your homes unharmed by war's annoy,
Your fields in hope's assurance sown,
   And harvested with songs of joy ;
Yet by that day of battle stern
Our city-circled shores may learn
   Free swords at need to draw,
Like them whose life-blood dyed the fern
   Of old at red Harlaw !

XVII.

THE FOUNDING OF THE FIRST SCOTTISH UNIVERSITY.

THE original institution of St. Andrews University took place in 1410, Bishop Henry Wardlaw, and the prior and chapter, being founders. The papal sanction, however, was not obtained until 1414, on the 3d of February in which year Henry de Ogilvie, Master of Arts, brought to St. Andrews the necessary privileges from Pope Benedict XIII. "On his happy arrival," says Bower, the continuator of Fordun, "the bells of all the churches in the city were set ringing; and on the following day (Sunday), the bulls were presented to the bishop, as chancellor, and read in presence of the whole clergy; after which 'Te Deum laudamus' was chanted. The rest of the day was passed in the most joyful manner, and during the night large fires were kept burning in the streets, while wine was drunk with gladness. On Tuesday there was a solemn procession to celebrate the arrival of the privileges, and also that of the relics of St. Andrew, which feast fell on that day. But who can describe that procession,

the sweet sounding chants of the clergy, the dances
of the people, and the pealing of organs? The
prior celebrated high mass, and the Bishop of Ross
preached. Four hundred clergy and members of
the convent, besides a wonderful multitude of lay
people, took part in the procession, to the glory of
God, and the praise and honour of the University."
The bulls were dated from Arragon, there being then
a schism in the Papacy, and Scotland adhering to
Pope Benedict; so that, in the following piece, the
expression "triple-crowned Rome" is not to be
taken literally. The language put into the mouth
of the "yeoman," regarding the repulse of Donald
of the Isles at Harlaw, in 1411, does not greatly
exaggerate the consequences which might have
attended a different result.

The Scottish Universities founded subsequently
to St. Andrews, were those of Glasgow, in 1450 ;
King's College, Aberdeen, 1495; Edinburgh, 1582 ;
and Marischal College, Aberdeen, 1593. I am not
aware that the foundation of any of them was
accompanied with such a fervour of popular joy as
in the case of the earliest University. That a warm
interest in academic institutions established in particular localities is not necessarily confined to the
educated classes, has been lately shewn in the place

where I write, in regard to the suppression of
Marischal College by a union (now carried out) of
the two local Universities and Colleges, and especially on the occasion of a "Head Court" of the
inhabitants of Bon-accord. Had the Government
scheme been defeated, the working men who were
present at that crowded meeting would probably
have celebrated the event by bonfires, and ringing
of St. Nicholas' bells.

XVII.

THE FOUNDING OF THE FIRST SCOTTISH UNIVERSITY.

HIGH unfurl the white cross banner,
　　Lift Saint Andrew's holy sign !
Lift the old white cross of Scotland,
　　Symbolling her faith divine !
Never yet in Scottish story
　　Dawned a brighter, prouder day ;
Never nobler theme of glory
　　Woke a Scottish minstrel's lay.

Fair the Dawn that o'er yon ocean
　　Travelled to our rocky shore,
When of old Saint Rule's high teaching
　　Cheered its gloom with heavenly lore.
Once again the mists are leaving,
　　And a brighter day begun ;
In its light our bosoms heaving,
　　Like yon billows in the sun !

Thus a youth of twenty summers
　　Chanted, as he held his way
On to where Saint Andrews' city
　　Rose beside its gleaming bay.
Flushed his cheek that daily, nightly
　　Studious toil and thought had paled ;
Flashed his eye in triumph brightly
　　As the minster's towers he hailed.

There the streaming white cross banner
　　Floats upon the breeze of morn ;
Thence afar the pealing music
　　Of rejoicing chimes is borne.
Well the glorious day beginneth,
　　When from triple-crowned Rome
Comes the mandate high that winneth
　　Learning her first Scottish home.

By that youth of twenty summers
　　Onward stepped his manly sire,
Grimly smiling as he listened
　　To the student's words of fire.
Scars were on his cheek, the token
　　Of the battle day that saw
Donald's ruthless Islesmen broken
　　On the field of fierce Harlaw.

Grimly smiling, spake the yeoman,—
    " Bells may chime and banners stream :
Little know I, yet this little,—
    Learning is no idle dream.
Ring the chimes then long and loudly,
    Yet remember, as they sound,
How the katerans, vaunting proudly,
— - Back were driven from Lowland ground.

" Brief the while since Donald's clansmen
    Poured in furious thousands down,
Wasting wide the northern Lowlands,
    Landward field and borough town.
All with thirst for plunder burning,
    Stirred to blood by frenzied bards,
Wit you well, for schools and learning
    Had those spoilers scant regards.

" Wit you truly, if our yeomen,
    Marching with the Lord of Mar,
Had not, in its onward rolling,
    Stemmed the fiery flood of war,—
Southward then its torrent sweeping,
    Hither had the savage foe
Rushed, no bounds to vengeance keeping,
    Kirk and homestead laying low.

"Then from heathery glens and mountains,
    Wilds that nurse the mighty Tay,
Wilder kerne in bands had gathered,
    Hastening down to share the prey :
Mute had been those chimes that, blending
    Past and present, tell the tale
How brave hearts, in fight contending,
    Saved the Lowlands from the Gael."

Joy was in Saint Andrews' city,
    Joy in cloister and in hall,
Priest and layman, lord and burgher,
    Keeping highest festival ;
Not for manhood's might achieving
    Trophies from red battle borne ;
Warfare's noblest triumph leaving
    Still some wounded heart to mourn.

Theirs was joy that Scotland's children
    Strangers' care would seek no more,
Happy in the kindly nurture
    Of her bosom's bounteous store :
France the fair no more should wile them
    Far beyond the waves of Forth ;
English tongues no more beguile them,
    Speaking lightly of the North.

Joy was in the ancient city,
　　Ever breaking from each tongue ;
With an ever-radiant gladness
　　Shone the face of old and young,
Brightly when at morn were starting
　　Into light the lofty spires,
Brightly when at day's departing
—— Spire-like burned the festal fires.

Banquets spread in old profusion,
　　Wine from brimming beakers poured ;
Full the feast, and free the welcome,
　　Free to burgher, priest, and lord !
Yea, when harp and lute are swelling,
　　Let the dance the hours employ :
Youth in every motion telling
　　Pulses of a common joy !

Joy was in Saint Andrews' minster,
　　Thronged from hallowed wall to wall ;
Heart and voice in glad thanksgiving
　　Lifted to the Lord of All.
Loud the rolling organ thundered,
　　Surging with the chant of praise
White-robed choir and priests four hundred
　　In their long procession raise.

Stole and cope and jewelled mitre,
  Crozier-staff and cross were there ;
Swung the censers, moved the banners
  Onward to the chancel fair :
Burst the song to God ascending,—
  "Glory in the highest be !
Peace on earth, and love unending
  Unto men from malice free !"

Thus they hailed the dawning brightness,
  Learning's dawn in Scottish land,
Hearts that for an age had mouldered,
  Ere the fiery zealot's hand
Smote the minster's walls so rudely,
  Ere fanatic feet had trod
O'er the carven work so goodly,
  Hallowed by their sires to God.

Onward from its early dawning
  On the rocky eastern shore,
Spread the light, as still were rising
  Homes of academic lore,
By the Clyde's yet quiet river,
  By the northern Don and Dee,
By the Forth, where, throned for ever,
  Rules the Lion land and sea.

Flourish all through coming ages,
　　Palaces of thought and truth !
Happy in their teachers' wisdom,
　　Happy in their guileless youth !
Double praise and blessing earning,
　　If this truth divine they prize,—
God's high will is truest learning,
　　- - And the good alone are wise !

XVIII.

THE SONG OF THE CAPTIVE KING.

ROBERT III., who knew and feared the ambition of his brother the Duke of Albany, became, after the murder of Rothesay, anxious that his only surviving son should be placed beyond danger of the like treatment. Prince James was accordingly, when in his fourteenth year, given in charge to certain trustworthy persons to be conveyed to France, there to prosecute his education. On the voyage, however, the vessel in which he sailed was seized by an English pirate, and the prince carried to the court of Henry IV. Although there was at the time a truce between the kingdoms, Henry most unwarrantably detained him as a captive or hostage, to the great grief of his bereaved father. The seizure of the prince took place on Palm Sunday, 1405. On the first anniversary of that day the heart-broken king died at Rothesay, the time and the place being associated with the loss of his two children. James, principally through the treasonable conduct of Albany, who is believed to have concerted the capture with Henry,

and who aimed at retaining and transmitting to his
own sons the government of Scotland, remained a
prisoner for the long period of nearly twenty years.
On the death of his father, he was proclaimed king
with the usual solemnities, although, to use the words
of Wynton,—

> "He was in England still,
> Holden all against his will,
> That he might of no kind wise
> Take any of his insigniis,
> As crown, sceptre, sword, and ring,
> Such as effeiris to a king."

The Duke of Albany affected the state of a
sovereign, and did all but assume the kingly title.
In his public documents he styled himself regent
"by the grace of God," and mentioned his "subjects."
While he discouraged any proposals for obtaining
the release of his king by negociation with England,
he exerted every effort to procure that of his own
son Murdoch, who had been taken prisoner at the
battle of Homildon, and who succeeded him in the
dukedom and regency. The government of the old
regent had been of the worst description, but his
son was as incapable of carrying on the business of
the state as of ruling his own family. "There is
a tradition, the simplicity of which seems to speak
its truth, that the regent had a favourite falcon,

which his son Walter had often requested unsuc-
cessfully, and at last, vexed with repeated refusal, he
tore it from his father's hand and twisted its neck ;
upon which Murdoch mildly exclaimed,—'Since you
pay me so little respect, I must invite him whom
both must obey.'" (Pinkerton's History of Scotland). Meanwhile James received from Henry's
care, as if in amends for his unjust detention, the
highest education in literature, art, and science, and
instruction in knightly exercises, that the country
could afford ; and his natural genius advanced him
to eminent rank among poets. Still the restraint
under which he was kept by Henry IV. and his
successor, must have been exceedingly irksome to a
prince so energetic and high-spirited. One is disposed to regret, on account of the many pleasant
associations connected with the younger Henry, that
the Scottish king was not indebted to him for his
freedom. It was not until 1424, soon after the
death of Henry V., that James was restored to his
country ; and the termination of his long captivity
was made the occasion of the greater joy to him by
his being united at the same time to the lady of his
heart. Not long before his release he composed the
" King's Quair" (or Book), the well known poem
which records his courtship of the beautiful Joanna

Beaufort, daughter of the Earl of Somerset, and cousin of Henry V. He describes himself as confined to his chamber in Windsor Castle, "in strait ward and in strong prison," but enjoying from his window, as well as a captive could, the view of the garden "fast by the tower's wall," and listening to the song with which "the little sweet nightingale" ushered in the bright May morning. It was then that he beheld his future queen walking forth with her two maidens to perform her morning orisons ;—

"The fairest and the freshest young flower
. That ever I saw, methought, before that hour ;"

and possessing, as he says,

"Beauty enough to make a world to dote."

The young king depicts her personal appearance in several stanzas marked with great beauty and delicacy of thought and expression ; and the whole poem, which is of considerable length, was a love-offering such as very few princes could bestow.

XVIII.

The Song of the Captive King.

Fair maiden of a noble line !
  Thy plighted love is sweet ;
One smile from thee, one glance divine,
  A bliss for monarchs meet ;
And fondly thus thy hand to press,
  Might life in death impart,
Yet never can I mourn the less
  A captive claims thy heart.

Though here at Henry's court so gay
  Be dwelling all delight ;
Though varied pleasures crowd the day,
  And song beguile the night ;
And I be free to love, O yet
  Not all that wealth can bring,
Nor love, shall wile me to forget
  That I amScotland's king !

A kingdom in the north is mine, ·
  A glorious mountain land,

But now the sceptre of my line
  Fills a usurper's hand ;
And from the day of grief that brought
  Death to my father dear,
Hath traitorous ambition wrought
  To keep me captive here.

_'Tis fitting that a prince be seen
  With all his peers around,
But princely style hath ever been
  To me an idle sound.
In vain for Douglas' form I look,
  Nor hear the corselets ring
Of chiefs whose tread of iron shook
  The halls of Scotland's king.

O maiden dear! it cannot be
  That treason's power should last,
And youth endure captivity
  Till strength and hope be past.
The strong shall sink, the proud shall fall,
  The faithful cease to grieve,
And soon within his royal hall
  Their exiled prince receive.

Then happy thousands, lady mine !
  Thy queenly form shall see,

And for that fairest face of thine
　My welcome gladder be ;
And songs of peace, poured gaily forth,
　Through all the land shall ring,
When thou art lady of the North,
　And James is Scotland's king.

XIX.

CATHARINE DOUGLAS.

ON the arrival of James I. in his own kingdom,
"great confluence of people," it is said by Boece,
"came to meet him out of all parts of Scotland,
right desirous to see him ; for many of them had
never seen him afore, or else, at least, the print of
his visage was out of their memory." From the
moment that his step was turned homewards he
began to study the course he was to pursue for the
punishment of those concerned in the usurpations
of his uncle's family, and for the restoration of
peace and security to his people. By evincing his
determination to make the proudest chiefs and
barons respect the laws, and by his vigilance in personally looking after the administration of justice
among all classes, he had proceeded a great way
towards the fulfilment of his resolution that "the
key should keep the castle, and the braken bush the
cow," when he became the victim of a dark con-
spiracy, the true motives for which are not well
known. It was organized by Sir Robert Graham, a

ruined and vindictive outlaw, Walter, Earl of Athol,
a son of Robert II., and Sir Robert Stewart, the
king's chamberlain and chief favourite. The plot
was carried into effect when the court was keeping
the festival of Christmas in the Dominican Monastery
at Perth, and on the night between the 20th and
21st of February 1437. To use the words of the
contemporary account first published in the appendix
to Pinkerton's History,—"they were occupied at
the playing of the chess, at the tables, in reading of
romances, in singing, piping and harping, and other
honest solaces, of great pleasure and disport.
Within an hour the king asked the voidee (the
grace-cup) and drank, and every man departed and
went to rest. Then Robert Stewart that was right
familiar with the king, and had all his command-
ments in the chamber, was the last that departed.
He knew well the false treason and consented there-
to, and therefore left the king's chamber doors open,
and had bruised and blundered the locks of them,
in such wise that no man might shut them ; and
about midnight he laid certain planks and hurdles
over the ditch that environed the garden of the
chamber, upon which entered the traitor Sir Robert
Graham, with a band of 300 persons." A young
maiden, Catharine Douglas, one of the Queen's

attendants, with a generous devotion which dis-
dained to consider the consequences to herself,
thrust her arm into the staple from which the bolt
of the chamber door had been removed, but the
feeble barrier thus interposed instantly gave way
before the violence of the conspirators, who rushed
into the apartment with weapons already stained
with the blood of a faithful page, Walter Straiton,
and murdered the king under circumstances of great
cruelty. Catharine Douglas was the daughter of
Sir William Douglas of Lochleven, and his wife
Marjory Lindsay, daughter of David, Earl of
Crawford, and, subsequently to the slaughter of
James (for "chronicles" are not altogether "mute"
on the point) was married to Alexander Lovell of
Bolunny. (Lord Lindsay's Lives of the Lindsays.
Boece's History.)

XIX.

CATHARINE DOUGLAS.

My lady and my love ! I know
  For thee 'tis sweetest joy to hear
My lay with beating heart rehearsed
  To thy sole listening ear,
When every star is bright above ;
Brightest of all, the star we love.

The broad full moon companioning,
  We marked its meeker beauty shine,
But she her fulness changing soon
  In fickle pale decline,
It turned its truer orb away,
To beam alone with brighter ray.

Fair names it hath, high names and old,
  From bards and sages here on earth,
And higher in the highest heaven
  That saw its beauteous birth :
To us that faithful light is known
By one dear name, " our star," alone.

High musings of a soul at rest
  Are ours, fair dreams of joy to come,
Fond thoughts that warmly swell the heart,
  But make affection dumb,
As silently, hand pressed in hand,
To watch our dearest star we stand.

All happy thoughts are mine, as thus
  I read with thee the starry skies;
And glancing oft with loving wile
  To watch thy thoughtful eyes,
What crowning of my love, to see
Their pure light fondly turned on me!

And now what noble theme of song
  Shall win to-night thy listening ear,
And flush thy fair young cheek with pride,
  My own, my only dear!
What new and not unworthy rhyme
Of Scotland's old historic time?

Lovedst thou the lay the poet king
  Sang in his weary golden thrall,
Ere Scotland hailed his glad return
  To freedom, home, and hall;
Ere James his own good sceptre swayed,
And lawless pride his power obeyed?

Sad was the lay ; a gentle grief
　　Like dawning joy was in its tone,
For love had o'er the captive's gloom
　　Sweet rays of promise thrown ;
But deeper woe must cloud the strain
That tells how royal James was slain.

Ah ! 'tis not thus, alone with thee,
　　Beneath yon loved and holy light,
My tongue would paint the cruelty
　　That stained the woful night,
Or speak the outlaw's name whose hand
To murder led the traitor band !

On thy pure lips a worthier name
　　Now softly trembles, maiden dear ;
Meeter for lips like thine to breathe,
　　And our pure star to hear :
Yes ! Catharine Douglas' noble deed
Hath earned full well such worthy meed.

Not Good Sir James, the Douglas old,
　　Had truer, readier arm than she
Who, for the bolt by treason drawn,
　　Of hers made offering free,
Despising mortal harm, to bring
A moment's safety to her king.

Sadly thy bosom sighs at thought
　　How that devoted arm was crushed
And broken in its faithfulness,
　　When James's murderers rushed,
And in his breast their daggers quivered,
Unarmed, unguarded, undelivered.

_That loyal lady did not die :
　　Though chronicles be mute of old,
And of her fortune and her fate
　　No history unfold,
Yet willing fancy shall for her
Become a happy chronicler.

The noble maiden perished not,
　　But lived the loved of all her kin ;
From all the land her faithfulness
　　Did praise and worship win ;
And they who hated Douglas' line
Yet loved the Lady Catharine.

Her loyalty and worth had laud
　　From high and low, from old and young,
And glowing minstrels duteously
　　Her brave devotion sung,
And suing barons bent the knee,
All for her worth and loyalty.

But one alone, a simple knight,
  Gallant in field and praised in hall,
Who loved her well and woo'd her long,
  She chose before them all,
And loving lived, for many a year,
His honoured dame and lady dear.

True love is wealth and purest gold,
  That knows no dimness or decrease ;
Solace in sorrow, joy in joy,
  Blessed content and peace ;
In memory a glory ever,
In hope and issue failing never.

True love is ours, my beauteous one !
  And shall no change or waning see,
But shine within our heart and home
  A guiding star to be ;
The light of love still shining on,
When sun and moon and stars are gone.

XX.

THE DOLE OF FLODDEN.

In August 1513, James IV. assembled his army on
the Borough moor, beside the Scottish capital, to the
number of nearly 100,000 men, for the purpose of
harassing the territories of his brother-in-law Henry
VIII., then personally engaged in the war in France
against Louis XII., whose chivalrous ally James
continued, when a more prudent policy would have
better pleased his own nobles, and saved the flower
of his people from a bloody grave. It was the
feigning voice of a woman that decided him. "The
queen of France," says Lindsay of Pitscottie, "writ
ane love letter to the king of Scotland, naming him
her love, shewing him that she had suffered meikle
rebuke for his sake in France, for the defending of
his honour; wherefore she believed that he wold
recompense her with some of his kingly support in
sic ane necessity, that is, that he wold raise ane
army and come three foot on English ground for her
sake ; and to that effect she sent him ane ring off
her finger, worth fifteen thousand French crowns."
(Chronicles of Scotland.) The Scottish host, which

M

in its progress to the Border dwindled away, from
scarcity of provisions and the unsteady disposition
of part of the troops, to 35,000 in number,
entered England on the 22d of August, and on
the 9th of the following month joined battle at
the hill of Flodden with the army of the Earl of
Surrey, numbering 26,000 men. On the next day,
when the rumour of the fatal result occasioned by
the rashness of King James reached Edinburgh, the
presidents, or temporary magistrates appointed to
act in the absence of the provost and bailies with
the host, issued a proclamation to the inhabitants of
the city, which forms one of the most interesting
entries in the contemporary Council Register. After
referring to "a great rumour now lately risen within
this town," but not yet verified, they commanded
"that all manner of personis nyhbours within the
samen, have reddy their fensabill gear and wapponis
for weir, and compeir thairwith to the said presidents,
at jowing of the common bell, for the keeping and
defens of the town against thaim that wald invade
the samen;" and also charged that all women of
the lower class "pass to their labours, and be not
seen upon the gait, clamourand and cryand, and the
other women of gude pass to the kirk and pray,
whan time requires, for our soverane lord and his

army." Lord Hailes remarks—" The magistrates of Edinburgh, when they issued this proclamation, must have been convinced that all was lost, and yet their orders are accurate and firm, without that pomp of words which, by studying to conceal fear, betrays it." To add to the distress of the city, a violent pestilence raged within it at the time of the battle of Flodden.

XX.

THE DOLE OF FLODDEN.

ROUND the old crags of Arthur's Hill
    The tearful mists are slowly creeping,
As dawns the morn, so sadly still,
    Dunedin's, Scotland's day of weeping.
Far murmurs from the city rise
Of wild distraction, mingled cries
    Of wailing and of fear :
Frequent and fast the war-bell tolls,
And up the misty mountain rolls
    Its burthen on the ear,
O'er ferny hollow, loch and lea
Replying to the moaning sea.

Alas for thee, Dunedin !   Woe
    For haughty Scotland's royal city !
In sorrow's depths now fallen so low,
    Thy foes might sigh for truest pity.
Though plague inhabit thee, and death
With pestilent and sickly breath
    The air of heaven oppress,

Where is the Scot that would forsake
Thy wall in fear, or shrink to take
    His part in thy distress,
When battle's ruin calls away
The strong to arm, the weak to pray ?

Last moon, on yonder moor so wide
⌐ (O 'twas a sight to banish sorrow !)
The day that witnessed Scotland's pride
    Half of its brightness seemed to borrow
From burnished mail and cloth of gold,
And princely banners high unrolled,
    From plume and helm and lance ;
While chimed with shout and charger's neigh
The clang of arms and trumpet's bray
    In warlike consonance ;
When James of Scotland marshalled forth
The best and bravest of the North.

Moan, moan, unquiet sea ! for thou
    Brought'st from the flattering South the token
Of honour then, of anguish now,
    And yet with honour's pledge unbroken.
Won by the gift of Beauty sent
With words of queenly blandishment ;
    Sworn on a lady's ring,

To challenge forth and to withstand
All England's power on English land ;
    Ah, hapless, hapless king !
Thy noble heart's blood's darker flow
Hath quenched that costly jewel's glow.

High were the strain that numbered o'er
    The thousands on the moor outspreading,
Their clans, their names and warlike store,
    The thousands to the Border treading !
King James beheld, with joyful eye,
The myriad pennons round him fly,
    The Lion-banner lead,
And felt a monarch's power and pride
To see his earls and barons ride
    Each on a barbed steed,
Their warriors bringing, at his will,
To fight for France at Flodden Hill.

So bright the martial splendour shone,
    So passed away like daylight dying,
That, when the last proud gleam was gone,
    Came shades of doubt, with tears and sighing.
And they who loved their king the most,
And shouted with the shouting host,
    For France made no acclaim,

Nor prayed for Scotland's arms good speed
With heart so fired as when at need
    Of liberty they came,
For right to strive, nor only try
A deed of boastful chivalry.

The grass upon the trampled plain
    Once more in its green strength was springing,
And days went by, of grief or gain
    No tidings from the Border bringing ;
Till some, that by the plague were stricken,
Told how strange sights would round them thicken
    Of banners wildly tost ;
And tender mothers woke and wept,
Dreaming at midnight, as they slept,
    That all they loved were lost :
They woke to hear, at morning's beam,
A waking rumour like their dream.

'Twas whispered in the Council hall
    At night, and louder told at morrow,
'Twas shrieked abroad at matin call
    Throughout the city, wild with sorrow,
That James of Scotland and his men,
His knights and earls, would ne'er again
    From Flodden Hill come back.

Then hearts were rent with sudden woe
In homes the lordly and the low,
    And one wide grief did rack
The nameless burgher's lonely mate,
And Margaret in her queenly state.

Hark in the crowded streets on high
    A voice proclaim 'mid shrieks and wailing !—
"Cease ye to clamour thus and cry,
    When firm resolve were more availing !
Ye faithful burghers, harnessed well,
Soon as ye hear the 'larum bell,
    The warning sound obey ;
And dames of worth, and matrons all,
That with your households weep in hall,
    Pass to the kirk and pray
That Heaven may yet our sovereign king,
And host, from woful peril bring !"

And lo ! while yet the dawn is grey,
    Frequent and fast the war-bell tolling,
Lead to God's house the mournful way
    The priests of God the All-consoling ;
With pale lips chanting, as they go,
"Out of the depths," a psalm of woe,
    A trembling, broken strain ;

And matrons old and maidens fair
With sad and faltering steps repair
    To swell the passing train,
In the deep chant of sorrow keeping
Their bitter part of moan and weeping.

DE PROFUNDIS.

Out of the dark and troubled deep
    Of sorrow, shame, and sin we call :
Lord, hear our cry ! the tears we weep
    For sin and shame and sorrow fall.

Dread God of wrath, what mortal may
    Thy frowning face behold and live !
Blest God of love, when sinners pray
    In faith and fear, Thou wilt forgive.

Thy promised blessing, Lord, to win,
    For peace and rest we look and long ;
And ere the watch of morn begin,
    To Thee our prayers for mercy throng.

O be Thou still Thy people's trust,
    And soon will sorrow vex no more ;
Soon will Thy mercy from the dust
    Of shame and sin our souls restore !

XXI.

QUEEN MAGDALENE.

SUDDEN as was the attachment which sprung up between the youthful James V. and Magdalene, the sole surviving daughter of Francis I., their marriage had been for years a favourite project of the Scottish government, and the repeated negociations with the king of France to that effect, begun so early as 1524, prepared the way for love. In the autumn of 1536, King James paid his visit to the French court, then at Lyons; and it is said by Lindsay of Pitscottie, that the beautiful princess, who appeared to be fading away with a hidden malady that gave the utmost anxiety to her royal father, "fra the time she saw the king of Scotland and spake with him, became so enamoured with him and loved him so weill, that she wold have no man alive to her husband but he allanerlie." James was twenty-five, and Magdalene in her seventeenth year when their marriage took place, on the 1st of January 1537, at Paris, in the Cathedral of Nôtre-Dame. From a contemporary painting, in the possession of Lord

Elgin, Miss Strickland has given an interesting
description of their appearance at the altar. "Magdalene is very lovely ; her features are small, regular,
and delicate ; her complexion fair, with light brown
hair, which is simply and becomingly arranged in
curls and plaits. She wears a small round cap,
formed of a network of pearls and jewels. She is
tall, slender and graceful in stature, with a long
throat elegantly moulded. Her countenance is indi-
cative of feminine sweetness and sensibility, and
there is something very maidenly in her attitude, as
she stands with downcast eyes, bending her head
slightly forward, and extending her hand to receive
the nuptial ring.—The bridegroom wears a short
full mantle of dark blue velvet, furred with sable,
and pantaloon hose of white satin. He is bare-
headed, very handsome, of a noble presence, and his
gay and spirited demeanour is quite in accordance
with his character."—(Lives of the Queens of Scotland). On Whitsuneve, 19th May 1537, they arrived
at Leith, welcomed with tumultuous joy by their
subjects. There is no incident in all history more
beautiful than Magdalene's behaviour at the moment
of her landing. "When the queen was come upon
earth," says Pitscottie, "she bowed her down to the
same and kissed the mould thereof, and thanked God

that her husband and she was come safe through the
seas." In the beginning of July following she died,
wept and bewailed by all the Scottish people, especially those who had so recently witnessed her
arrival ; and "the king's heavy moan that he made
for her was greater than all the rest."—(Lindsay's
Chronicles.)

XXI.

QUEEN MAGDALENE.

A LILY pure was Magdalene,
  Of France the love and pride,
Alone before the altar cross
  Kneeling at morning tide.

Her cheek was pale, but not with grief,
  Her eye undimmed by tears ;
The deadly ill that wore her youth
  Had brought no dying fears.

For ne'er had courtly pleasures held
  Her saintly soul in thrall ;
The solace of a holy hymn
  In worth excelled them all.

And there, in guileless maidenhood,
  The princess knelt to pray
That soon her happy hour might come
  To die and pass away.

Then to her bower went Magdalene,
   In beauty without peer,
And thither came her loving sire,
   King Francis, blithe of cheer.

" Sweet morrow to my lily fair,
   My daughter dear and true !
There waits a noble prince for thee,
   Come from afar to woo."

By word or look she answered not,
   But meekly stept in hall,
Where Scotland's king, of manly port,
   Low on his knee did fall.

" Lily of France, fair Magdalene ! "
   Thus 'gan the prince to sue,
And straight a strangely winning power
   Her maiden bosom knew.

She saw a form, she heard a voice,
   That changed and charmed away
The marble paleness of her cheek
   That hour and all the day ;

For all the day the charm, the power
   Of love's enduring life
With mortal ill victoriously
   Maintained a glowing strife.

And loved and loving, as she knelt
   At eventide to pray,
No more her spirit sighed from earth
   In youth to pass away.

But fate's cold whisper came unsought,—
   "Thine hour is near to die!"
Ah, then her cheek's pure radiance paled,
   And tear-drops dimmed her eye!

All that is earthly shameth not
   The eyes that watch unseen,
Those Angel eyes that smiled on her,
   The loving Magdalene!

From Nôtre-Dame at sunny morn
   The bells o'er Paris rang;
In Nôtre-Dame the choristers
   A joyful anthem sang;

For there was beauty mated well,
    With love's thrice blessed ring ;
The darling and the pride of France
    With Scotland's noble king.

When she had breathed a parting prayer
    In chapel all alone,
And shed a last unplaining tear
    Upon the altar stone,

Her dearest lord she whispered low,—
    " Though France may fairer be,
For home, my heart is sick for home,
    In Scotland and with thee !"

And sped with blessings, blest with prayers,
    Love gifts in priceless store,
She parted, to return again—
    Ah never, never more !

Sailing with him, her only love,
    With longing eyes she stood
To view from far the rocky heights
    That watch o'er Holyrood.

Ho ! gather ye who love King James !
    In ready welcome throng ;
And cry, " Long live Queen Magdalene !"
    So shall her days be long.

She sighed, she smiled that shout to hear,
    And lifting from the strand
Its pebbles to her lips in love,
    She blessed her husband's land.

And for her words so kindly sweet,
    Rose louder to the sky
The shout, " Long live Queen Magdalene !"
    The Queen who came to die.

For summer's breeze, that sped her bark,
    Yet sighed in wold and wood,
When she with holy psalms was laid
    To rest in Holyrood.

XXII.

LAMENT OF THE COMMONS FOR JAMES THE FIFTH.

THE body of the Scottish people might well lament the early death of James V., looking forward as they did to a long minority of the sovereign, since the heir to the throne was the infant Princess Mary. He was removed in the midst of labours which had for their end the welfare of Scotland, and the amelioration of the condition of his poorer subjects. For the vigorous measures which he took to effect these objects, many of the powerful and turbulent nobles hated his government, and disliked himself. The obstacles often thrown in his way by them vexed his spirit ; their haughty disobedience of his commands at Fala Muir filled him with anger ; and the subsequent disgraceful rout at Solway Moss wounded his own and his country's honour, and broke his heart. At Linlithgow, in 1541, " whilst he lay a-sleeping," says Archbishop Spottiswoode, "he imagined that Sir James Hamilton, whom he caused to be executed, came unto him with a drawn sword in his hand, and therewith cut off both his arms, threatening within a short time to return and de-

prive him of his life. With this he awaked, and as
he lay musing what the dream could import, news
were brought him of the death of his two sons,
James and Arthur, who died at St. Andrews and
Stirling, at one and the very same hour. The next
year, which was the year of our Lord 1542, being
overwhelmed with grief and passion for the loss his
army received at Solway, he departed this life, at
Falkland, in the 32d year of his age. Some few
days before he died, he had advertisement that his
queen was delivered of a daughter at Linlithgow ;
at which time, it is said, he burst forth in passion,
saying, ' It came with a lass (meaning the crown),
and will go with a lass ; lie upon it ! ' After which,
he was not heard to utter many words." (Hist. of
Church and State of Scotland.)   James was called
in his own time the "King of the Commons ;" and
popular tradition has preserved several anecdotes
connected with his occasional wanderings through
the country,—

> " After the fashion of the time
> And humour of the golden prime
> Of good Haroun Alraschid."

The deeds of Wallace Wight are not more
generally known than the adventures of the " Gude-
man of Ballangeich."

XXII.

LAMENT OF THE COMMONS FOR JAMES THE FIFTH.

THERE'S sighing and sorrow the wide Lowland
    thorough,
And low droops the banner on Falkland's proud
    wall,
For James, the free-hearted, our Prince, has departed,
The king of broad Scotland lies dead in his hall.

And there as he's shrouded, with stern brows o'er-
    clouded,
His barons are gathered in gloomiest show ;
But false is their seeming, and shame on their
    scheming
That broke his high heart with dishonour and woe !

By Fala's retreating, and Solway's defeating
'   Sad Scotland has witnessed their treason in field :
From pride that would rend her Heaven's mercy
    defend her !
Our land from her nobles deliver and shield !

But true is their sorrow, the wide Lowland thorough,
Who waken to toil with the dawning of day ;

For now long and dreary oppression shall weary
    The landless and poor when their king is away.

Their roofs have received him, their welcome re-
    lieved him
    From wandering unknown in the moorland by
    night,
When far he went roaming alone in the gloaming,
    Or ranging at will in the merry moonlight,

And oft to their guisings and homely rejoicings
    He came a poor minstrel, or forester free ;
Where mirth notes were waking, or lone hearts were
    breaking,
    The blithest, the best, and the kindest was he.

Their love he sought ever where courtiers came
    never,
    And kinglike in council he wrought for their
    weal :
Their homage was purest, their aid was the surest ;
    He knew that the lowly had aye been the leal.

And sighing for sorrow the wide Lowland thorough,
    With darker foreboding his worth we recall :
When sorest we need him, no son to succeed him,
    The King of the Commons lies dead in his hall.

XXIII.

THE FLIGHT FROM LOCHLEVEN.

THE escape of Queen Mary from Lochleven Castle, where she was imprisoned in June 1567 by the barons confederated for her dethronement, occurred on the evening of the 2d of May in the following year. The castle belonged to William Douglas, and from its insular situation, as well as the character of its owner, was considered by the leaders of the revolution to be completely secured against such a casualty. George Douglas, the laird of Lochleven's younger brother, having become devoted to her interest, had once nearly succeeded in an attempt to accomplish her freedom ; but the queen, who had disguised herself as a menial servant, was discovered by the whiteness of her hands, and carried back to more strict confinement. Young Douglas was dismissed from the castle, but being earnestly bent on the deliverance of his beauteous sovereign, he concerted measures with Lord Seton and the Hamiltons, and with the assistance of " Willie," a page at the castle, effected his purpose in the manner narrated in the ballad. The particulars are minutely given in a statement drawn up at the time from the information of John Beaton, a gentleman actively concerned in the scheme, and since their publication by Mr. Tytler (Hist., vol. vii. app. No. 7,) have taken the place of the well-known story previously received. Without a moment's delay after the queen reached the shore, she was furnished with a horse, rode to the Frith of Forth, and crossing at the ferry arrived at Niddry Castle, and shortly afterwards proceeded to Hamilton, where she found herself in the midst of powerful friends.

XXIII.

THE FLIGHT FROM LOCHLEVEN.

WHY steps in hall, with brow so stern,
　　Lochleven's island lord?
Why keeps dark Douglas night and noon
　　Unceasing watch and ward?

His arm against our Mary's right
　　Upholds false Moray's power;
And Scotland's Queen a captive weeps
　　Within his gloomy tower.

But matched with daring loyalty
　　All prison bars are vain,
And loyal hearts shall hail her soon
　　Set free from prison pain.

The castle bell rings o'er the lake,
　　As smiles the westering sun;
And ere the first pale star come forth
　　Her freedom shall be won!

For one true heart in yonder keep
   Beats high that sound to hear ;
Firm be his courage, prompt his hand,—
   Their trial time is near !

Right cheerly sounds the castle bell
   To board and cup to call
The warder from his lonely watch,
   And household one and all.

And "bar the gate !" proud Douglas cries ;
   " Bring hither ale and wine :
Nor knight nor lord shall rouse from board
   The meanest knave of mine !"

The gate is barred, the baron sups,
   The castle key beside :
Who 'scapes without its secret aid
   Across the lake may ride !

And ready at the baron's call
   Attends a little page,
Who fills him up the sparkling cup
   That gladdens youth and age.

But 'ware the page, Sir Castellan !
    Of cunning hand is he :
The wine-cup on the board he leaves,
    But not the castle key !

'Tis won ! 'tis won ! O thought of joy,
    Of joy and chilling fear !
And soon as forth from presence gone,
    His step outstrips the deer.

Well may he speed with throbbing heart,
    And lightly bounding limb ;
The fairest lady of the land
    In chamber waits for him !

And proudly may his fingers fold
    Around the burly key ;
For Scotland's Queen is captive yet,
    And he shall set her free !

She listens for his hurrying feet,
    She hears his quickening breath,
And pale, beside the chamber door,
    She leans, as still as death.

But with a glance she questions him,
    If he have freedom brought :
His joyful eyes and loaded hand
    Make answer to her thought.

Dark Douglas at the wine-cup sits,
    Dreaming of praise and power,
While Mary, flushed with hope, forsakes
    Her gloomy prison bower.

Her little maiden's trembling hand
    She takes with gentle care,
As o'er the silent stones they pass,
    And down the winding stair.

Turned by the page, the noisy key
    Has smote unto her heart,
That in a deep-drawn sigh is driven
    Nigh from all hope to part ;

But joy, O joy ! the free wind comes
    To bathe her weary eyes ;
And at her feet the ready boat
    Upon the water lies.

O prosper well the gallant ship
  Which crossed the ocean brine,
To bring the wary Castellan
  That cup of sparkling wine !

But ah ! that hands of matchless white,
  That Scotland's sceptre bore,
Should now be straining wearily
  The hard and rugged oar !

The queenly lady and the page
  Together bend and row,
And past the tower's long shadow soon
  With freer hearts they go.

" Look round thee to the shore," she cries,
  " My bright eyed maid, and see
If mounted horsemen to the lake
  Approach by rock or tree."

" O lady ! riding bravely down,
  A troop of knights appears :
Between the wood and water move
  Their starry twinkling spears.

"Two nobles with their plumes of white
　　The mounted spearmen lead,
And one into the lake, O look !
　　Has spurred his prancing steed."

"Then cheer thee well, my gallant page,
　　And stoutly ply the oar !
Lord Seton and young Douglas wait
　　To welcome us on shore.

" Adieu, disloyal Castellan !
　　Adieu, unlovely tower !
Thy walls are dark and joyless all,
　　Nor meet for lady's bower.

" Ply well the oar ! our friends are nigh,
　　Their steeds are wondrous fleet,
And princely halls will open wide
　　Their welcome Queen to greet.

" For there are hearts in Scotland yet
　　That burn for Mary's wrong,
And carls and knights and yeomen true
　　Will round her banner throng !"

XXIV.

THE BATTLE OF LANGSIDE.

ON Mary's restoration to freedom, her friends crowded in considerable numbers to her assistance, and a bond for the restitution of her authority was speedily signed by nine earls, nine bishops, eighteen lords, twelve abbots and priors, and nearly one hundred lesser barons. She encamped her army at Hamilton, and the Regent Moray, who was at the time in Glasgow, not many miles distant, lost not a moment in summoning a force to oppose the Queen. He had the advantage of the military skill of Sir William Kirkaldy of Grange, who commanded his cavalry, but who, only five years afterwards, died in the cause of Mary by the hands of the executioner. A brief but decisive engagement took place on 13th May 1568, at Langside, where the Queen's troops were encountered on their way from Hamilton towards Dumbarton. On beholding her troops completely routed, Mary rode with the utmost speed to the Abbey of Dundrennan, in Galloway, about sixty miles from Langside, and near the English

territory.   She there adopted the fatal resolution of
seeking refuge in England, thus throwing herself
into the power of her enemy, Queen Elizabeth, who
thenceforward treated her as a prisoner, and after
repeatedly changing the place of her captivity, and
increasing its severity, during the long period of
nearly nineteen years, at last put her to death by
the executioner's axe in the castle of Fotheringay.

XXIV.

THE BATTLE OF LANGSIDE.

At eve by broad Lochleven,
   An eve in gladsome May,
A grey-haired minstrel sat and sang
   A new and joyous lay.

He saw the torches twinkle
   Within the island tower,
And sang how Mary, Scotland's queen,
   Had 'scaped false Moray's power.

But came a sound that startled
   The still and lonely place :
Behind him to the lake advanced
   A courser's clanging pace.

His side was red with spurring,
   And white with foam his mane,
And travel-stained the trooper's form
   Who grasped the bridle rein.

Close by the waveless water
　The bridle back he drew;
His bugle horn he lifted thrice,
　And thrice a blast he blew.

Answered the castle warder
　In winded echoes three,
That cast upon the summer night
　A wandering melody.

" What news, what news, bold trooper ! "
　The merry harper cried :
" O joyful is the news I bring,"
　The horseman quick replied.

" The noble Earl of Moray
　Hath foiled the Popish Queen,
And fair Langside, by Glasgow town,
　A goodly slaughter seen."

Then sighed the aged harper,
　O'erta'en with sudden woe :
" How now ! " the angry trooper spake ;
　" Hear'st thou my tidings so ?

" If thou art Rome's abettor,
    Or kneel'st at Mary's shrine,
Then will the news be hard to bear
    As purgatory's pine!"

" I hold not Rome's delusion,
    Yet Mary's right confess,
-For change of creed shall never make
    My loyalty the less.

" But come you from the battle?"
    " Straight from the fight I come :
Six thousand were Queen Mary's men,
    And four our gallant sum.

" Her vassals through the greenwood
    This morn had weened to go,
But knightly Grange their purpose marked,
    And sorely marred their show.

" ' Go win,' he cried, ' ye troopers,
    The river's southern side,
Each horseman with a haghuttcer !'
    And so we crossed the Clyde.

" Then perished many a foeman,
    From bloody saddle thrown
By thickening shots our marksmen sent
    From bank, and bush, and stone.

" Then pike with pike, and hagbut
    To hagbut closely set,
With steed to steed, and hand to hand,
    The hosts in battle met.

" 'Tis said that your Queen Mary
    At distance spied the fray :
She saw her mightiest nobles flee,
    Ere passed one hour away ;

" The Hamiltons, the Setons,
    Argyll and all his men ;
Nor soon will Mary's charms recall
    Their broken bands again.

" Let her go rue her beauty
    In sober convent weeds !
In convent cell her Aves tell,
    Or lovers, on her beads ! "

Thus spake the hasty trooper,
　The harper mutely heard,
But bitter sorrow and disdain
　His loyal spirit stirred.

Uprose he, unreplying,
　His weary way to go :
And evermore his harp was strung
　To melodies of woe.

XXV.

DIRGE FOR MARY STUART.

At Fotheringay, on the 8th of February 1587, Mary fell a sacrifice to the fears of Elizabeth. With the dignity of a queen and the composure of a Christian, as her severest judges confess, she died as one conscious of none of the crimes laid to her charge. She was indeed more sinned against than sinning. "As thine arms, Lord Jesus, were stretched out upon the Cross, so receive me within the arms of thy mercy!" Such was part of her last prayer at the block : the thought she expressed being probably drawn from a Latin hymn familiar and dear to her, and which has been thus rendered :—

> " As now the sun's declining rays
>   Towards the eve descend,
>   E'en so our years are sinking down
>   To their appointed end.
>
> " Lord, on the cross thine arms were stretched,
>   To draw us to the sky ;
>   O grant us then that cross to love,
>   And in those arms to die!"

"May God," she said, "forgive those who have

sought my death ! The Judge of the secret thoughts
and actions of men knows my heart. He knows that
I have always desired the union of Scotland and
England." After the execution, the corpse was
treated with gross indignity, but in the verses it is
assumed that at least before her funeral, under the
directions of Elizabeth, more decency was observed
towards the remains of the Scottish Queen. In the
person of her son, James VI., a union of the crowns
such as she prayed for did take place, and great
prosperity and happiness have resulted to both
kingdoms, but only after the lapse of many miserable
years of national trouble. It may have been, that
those times of fear and calamity were ordained by
the providence of Heaven, in order that such a
union should not produce its natural advantages,
until the blood of Mary Stuart, which cemented it,—
the great iniquity committed by the ruler of one
country, and secretly approved of by the chief men
of the other,—had been atoned for by the united
nations.

XXV.

DIRGE FOR MARY STUART.

REST to Queen Mary, sweetest rest!
    Peace to the soul whose peace was slain!
Joy to the spirit sorrow-prest,
    Eternal joyance, glorious gain!

Sweet rest to her who shrouded lies
    Where tapers wane at dawning day,
And mourners fill with bursting sighs
    The blood-stained hall of Fotheringay!

Lift not the shroud!   A speaking stain
    Of blood upon its sable seen,
Tells how the spirit fled from pain,
    For there the headsman's axe has been.

Beside their slaughtered lady dear
    The faithful few have moaned and wept,
And all the night their vigil drear,
    Through all the ghostly night, have kept.

Why grieve they thus ?   Love never weeps
  For captives won from thrall forlorn ;
And she who there so calmly sleeps
  Captivity's long pain has borne.

Why mourn for her ?   Ah, mourn the dead !
  Though pain depart in mortal sleep,
Still must the tear of love be shed,
  Still must the living wail and weep.

Lament, O France, for Mary's doom !
  Her heart's dear country, from the time
A child she saw thy gardens bloom,
  And shared thy crown in beauty's prime :

Land in whose language best each word
  For hope, or joy, or love, she knew ;
Whose name remembered freshly stirred
  The anguish of her last adieu !

And thou, wide Scotland, wail ! for she
  Was born sole heir to Scotland's crown,
When James, from all his royalty,
  In sorrow to the grave went down.

Swell high the dirge for Scotland's Queen !
　Ye minstrels of the north arise,
If but one virtue that has been
　Yet in your boasted harping lies !

Seek not to rouse your native land
　To vengeance due for England's deed,
Whose queen with an unholy hand
　Had doomed a Queen of Scots to bleed.

Soon will the dark Avenger shake
　That sceptred hand with palsy fear,
That proud and stony bosom quake
　The hollow voice of Death to hear.

Bid not the daring Borderer come
　England to foray wide and far ;
Wake not the gathering lowland drum
　Nor wing the fiery cross of war.

King Robert's heart is dead and sere,
　Dim is the blade wight Wallace bore,
The Douglas lies in charnel drear,
　And Flodden's Knight returns no more.

Though Mary's son your homage claim,
　　His heart is weak, his love is cold :
A moment's wrath his cheek may flame,
　　But to her foes his thoughts are sold.

Ye minstrels ! wake a softer string,
　　Avenging battle's notes forego,
And Mary's changeful story sing,
　　Her birth, her beauty, and her woe.

Their rocky hearts and hate subdue
　　Who stained with blood her palace bower,
Shamed her with scorning, and o'erthrew
　　With cruel grasp her queenly power.

O tell how, with her parting breath
　　Forgiving all, Queen Mary died,
And, ere her lips grew dumb in death,
　　Her truth she meekly testified.

To hear her sad departing sung
　　The sternest eye a tear may shed ;
Fanatic passion's fiery tongue
　　Less fiercely blame the silent dead ;

And future Scots will sighing say,
    In some far time from trouble free,
Ah, that our wiser, happier day
    Had owned a flower so fair as she !

XXVI.

THE UNION SONG.

LONG time in the rude stormy ages of old,
  The Scot and the Southron were strangers and foes,
And oft at their meeting on rampart and wold
  Hath clanged the harsh discord of battle and blows.

Now smiling in verdure their battle-fields lie,
  And Britons meet Britons as aliens no more,
For bound in a Union majestic and high
  Their hearts have forgotten the rancour of yore.

Fair England, thy Rose hath its bloom from above,
  Thy Thistle, proud Scotland, is strong on its stem,
And long-parted Erin, thy union of love
  Adds strength to thy beauty and honour to them.

The leaves of thy Shamrock, green isle, shadow forth,
  As threefold and free in the sunlight they grow,
How flourish united the lands of the North ;
  They share but one fortune, one nurture they know.

Unchanging in love and unfailing in might,
  The honour of one is the glory of all,
For ever rejoicing in liberty's light,
  And ready, aye ready at liberty's call.

The Flag of their Union far o'er the wide earth
  Is welcomed with gladness; and ne'er may it cease
To wave as the emblem of valour and worth,
  Proclaiming in battle the promise of peace!

Let peace and goodwill be its mission divine,
  And angels above shall its conquests record,
While the world shall confess, not in vain we combine
  Threefold on our banner the Cross of the Lord.

Though bright be the trophies our fathers have won
  In thought's high achievement and manhood's
      emprize,
We'll rest not our fame on the days that are gone,
  Or boast us the sons of the brave and the wise.

The children shall equal the deeds of the sire,
  The future in glory out-glory the past;
And dearly we'll cherish, till Time shall expire,
  One Country, one Cause, and one Hope at the last!

SHORTLY after the accession of James VI. to the
throne of England in 1603, he issued a proclamation,
requiring that all his subjects in Great Britain should
bear on their ships' flags "the Red Cross, commonly
called St. George's Cross, and the White Cross,
commonly called St. Andrew's Cross, joined together." When the kingdoms were united in 1707,
this emblem was formally adopted, and at the
union with Ireland in 1801, a third cross, the
red saltire of St. Patrick, was added to the flag of
the empire. Thus was formed what is known as
the Union Jack. *Quis separabit?* Such is the
motto of the Order of St. Patrick. Were separation
possible it would be foolish to wish for it. Let Scotland, for her part, be proud of having in old times
nobly vindicated her rights in contest with England,
a country so much superior in extent and other
natural advantages, but she may be prouder still of
her voluntary union with her ancient foe. We are
Scots by name, but Britons by surname. If the
one country has ceased to be independent, so has
the other, for mutual support is essential to the well-
being of either. We are not English, however,
although we are Britons. I have therefore no
liking for the schemes of those who denounce the

maintenance of any distinctive national feeling as an antiquated absurdity. When a Scot ceases to love Scotland as such—as the same Scotland which existed centuries before any union was dreamt of—he will have little independence of character left. Attachment to a place merely on account of the comforts or position we enjoy, or even for the sake of those we love in it, is not patriotism. Our country is the land which God has given us, and He has bestowed also that consciousness of individual responsibility which incites the real patriot to do what in him lies to advance the interest and reputation of his native soil. "Whatsoever things are true, whatsoever things are honest, whatsoever things are just, whatsoever things are pure, whatsoever things are lovely, whatsoever things are of good report; if there be any virtue, and if there be any praise;" they are all fostered by the maintenance of a national spirit.

ADDITIONAL NOTES.

P

ADDITIONAL NOTES.

———————

I.

BALLAD OF SIR PATRICK SPENS.

Considering the general subject of the present volume,
I shall not be going far out of my way in making
some remarks on this ballad, the genuineness of which
as a relic of the ancient minstrelsy of Scotland has been
called in question. Its chief impugner is Mr. Robert
Chambers, who has gone the length of attempting to
shew that, along with upwards of a score of other popular
Scottish ballads, it is the composition of Lady Wardlaw,
the author of "Hardyknute."* The following observa-
tions in support of the antiquity of "Sir Patrick Spens,"
and bearing also on the genuineness of numerous pro-
ductions belonging to the same department of the
poetical literature of Scotland, are almost identical with

———————

* The Romantic Scottish Ballads : their Epoch and
Authorship ; being the First of a Series of Edinburgh Papers,
by Robert Chambers, F.R.S.E, F.S.A.S., F.G.S., F.L.S., etc.,
Author of "Traditions of Edinburgh." William and Robert
Chambers, London and Edinburgh, 1859. (Pp. 46.)

some offered by way of answer in a pamphlet published
shortly after the appearance of Mr. Chambers's paper.*
I need not make further allusion here to the ill-
advised theory of a particular authorship.

The ballad in question was printed in Percy's
"Reliques of Ancient English Poetry," in 1765, "from
two MS. copies transmitted from Scotland," but that
editor was able to furnish only eleven stanzas. As
many more were supplied by Sir Walter Scott, in the
"Minstrelsy of the Scottish Border" (1802). Scott
also took his version "from two MS. copies," and he
says—"That the public might possess this curious
fragment as entire as possible, the editor gave one of
these copies, which seems the most perfect, to Mr.
Robert Jamieson, to be inserted in his collection."
We accordingly find it in Jamieson's "Popular Ballads
and Songs, from tradition, manuscript, etc." (1806.)
Another variety appeared in Peter Buchan's "Ancient
Ballads and Songs of the North of Scotland" (1828).
Buchan tells us—"It was taken down from the recitation of a wight of Homer's craft, who, as a wandering
minstrel, blind from his infancy, has been travelling in
the north as a mendicant for these last fifty years.
He learned it in his youth from a very old person, and
the words are exactly as recited, free from those

* The Romantic Scottish Ballads, and the Lady Wardlaw
Heresy. A. Brown and Co., Aberdeen, 1859. (Pp. 49.)

emendations which have ruined so many of our best Scottish ballads." A comparison of the versions of Percy, Scott, Jamieson, and Buchan, so numerous are the variations in the language and construction, not one stanza being exactly the same as another, should suffice to prove that the ballad had a popular origin, and had been handed down by oral tradition through many generations.*

---

* In the latter of the two pamphlets referred to, these versions are, for the sake of easy comparison, printed side by side. I may give here the last collated version from " The Ballads of Scotland," edited by Professor Aytoun, but have pleasure in stating, that since the publication of the second edition of that work, so happily executed, Mr. Aytoun has obtained yet another copy of the ballad, taken down from the recitation of an aged person, and differing in several respects from any previously recovered.

> The king sits in Dunfermline toun,
>   Drinking the blude-red wine ;
> "O whaur shall I get a skeely skipper,
>   To sail this ship of mine ?"

> Then up and spake an eldern knight,
>   Sat at the king's right knee ;
> " Sir Patrick Spens is the best sailor
>   That ever sailed the sea."

> The king has written a braid letter,
>   And seal'd it with his hand,
> And sent it to Sir Patrick Spens,
>   Was walking on the sand.

I will now bring together the principal arguments
stated for the modern authorship of "Sir Patrick Spens;"
and in doing so in the words of Mr. Chambers, a writer

"To Noroway, to Noroway,
    To Noroway o'er the faem;
The king's daughter to Noroway,
    It's thou maun tak' her hame."

The first line that Sir Patrick read,
    A loud laugh laughed he,
The next line that Sir Patrick read,
    The tear came to his e'e.

"O wha is this has done this deed,
    This ill deed done to me,
To send us out at this time o' the year
    To sail upon the sea?"

They hoisted their sails on a Monday morn,
    Wi' a' the haste they may;
And they hae landed in Noroway
    Upon the Wodensday.

They hadna been a week, a week,
    In Noroway but twae,
When that the lords o' Noroway
    Began aloud to say—

"Ye Scotismen spend a' our king's gowd,
    And a' our queenis fee."
"Ye lie, ye lie, ye liars loud,
    Sae loud's I hear ye lie!

whose studies have lain so much in this department of
literature, I give abundant advantage to the upholders
of that theory. Mr. Chambers urges "the want of

"For I brought as much o' the white monie,
    As gane my men and me,
And a half-fou o' the gude red gold,
    Out owre the sea with me.

"Be't wind or weet, be't snaw or sleet,
    Our ship shall sail the morn."
"Now ever alack, my master dear,
    I fear a deadly storm.

"I saw the new moon late yestreen,
    Wi' the auld moon in her arm ;
And I fear, I fear, my master dear,
    That we shall come to harm !"

They hadna sailed a league, a league,
    A league but barely three,
When the lift grew dark, and the wind blew loud
    And gurly grew the sea

The ropes they brak, and the top-masts lap,
    It was sic a deadly storm ;
And the waves came o'er the broken ship,
    Till a' her sides were torn.

"O whaur will I get a gude sailor
    Will tak' the helm in hand,
Until I win to the tall top-mast,
    And see if I spy the land ?"

any ancient manuscript, the absence of the least trait of
an ancient style of composition, the palpable modern-
ness of the diction—for example, 'our ship must sail

"It's here am I, a sailor gude,
    Will tak' the helm in hand,
Till ye win to the tall top-mast,
    But I fear ye'll ne'er spy land."

He hadna gane a step, a step,
    A step but barely ane,
When a bolt flew out of the gude ship's side,
    And the salt sea it cam' in.

"Gae, fetch a web of the silken claith,
    Another o' the twine,
And wap them into the gude ship's side,
    And let na the sea come in."

They fetched a web o' the silken claith,
    Another o' the twine,
And they wapp'd them into the gude ship's side,
    But aye the sea came in.

O laith, laith were our gude Scots lords
    To weet their leathern shoon,
But lang ere a' the play was o'er,
    They wat their heads abune.

O lang, lang may the ladies sit,
    Wi' their fans into their hand,
Or e'er they see Sir Patrick Spens
    Come sailing to the land.

the faem,' a glaring specimen of the poetical language
of the reign of Queen Anne,—and still more palpably,
of several of the things alluded to, as cork-heeled shoon,
hats, fans, and feather-beds, together with the inapplicableness of the story to any known event of actual
history :" and he particularly insists that " no old poet
would use foam as an equivalent for the sea ; but it
was just such a phrase as a poet of the era of Pope
would love to use in that sense." Still further, he
declares that the ballad (as it appears in Percy's
" Reliques") is " so rounded and complete, so free moreover from all vulgar terms," that he is almost confident
it is printed in the condition in which it was left by
the author.

" The want of any ancient manuscript " can be no
argument against the antiquity of a poem, versions of
which have been obtained from oral recitation, otherwise the great mass of ballads of all kinds collected by
Scott, and by others since his time, must lie under

O lang, lang may their ladies sit,
  Wi' their gowd kaims in their hair,
A' waiting for their ain dear lords,
  For them they'll see nae mair.

Half owre, half owre to Aberdour,
  It's fifty fathom deep,
And there lies gude Sir Patrick Spens,
  Wi' the Scots lords at his feet.

equal suspicion. Bannatyne, in the sixteenth century, and Allan Ramsay, in the early part of the eighteenth, were not collectors of popular poetry in the same sense as those who have since been so active in that field. The former contented himself, for the most part, with transcribing the compositions of Dunbar, Henrysone, and other " makers" well known by name, and Ramsay took the bulk of his " Evergreen" from Bannatyne's MS. That a great many poems of the ballad class, afterwards collected and printed, must have been current among the people when the " Evergreen" was published, no one that knows anything of the subject will deny. The knowledge that Percy was engaged with his work led to his receiving copies of several Scottish pieces, and amongst them " Sir Patrick Spens." The reputation which the " Reliques" obtained, induced a search for other remains of the unwritten poetry of Scotland. " The absence of the least trait of an ancient style of composition" is next urged by the objector. The whole appearance of the ballad is completely in accordance with a popular origin, and subsequent preservation by oral tradition. The very " want of any ancient manuscript" accounts for what the objector calls its modern look, as it does for the great difference between the several versions. The style of " Sir Patrick Spens" is not essentially different from that of old ballad poetry of the same class. From the earliest times, every event

in which the people took an interest appears to have
been made the subject of a ballad or song, varying in
form as in length. For many generations after the in-
vention of printing, there existed two kinds of such
poetry, one purely traditionary, and the other passing
through the press. In the sixteenth century pedantry
characterised nearly every work of the pen, and where
this feature was wanting its place was supplied by one
much less tolerable. The age that could relish the
scurrilous "flytings" of Dunbar and Kennedy was not
likely to appreciate or take an interest in the purer and
simpler ballads of the people, which, owing to the
humble position of their authors, were not put into the
hands of the printer, and did not require such aid to
preserve them from one generation to another, among
thousands who had nothing else to engage their minds
in the intervals of their daily labour and their religious
duties. Take, in illustration of these remarks, the black
letter poems transmitted to the English court from time
to time during the reign of Queen Mary of Scotland, by
persons in the interest of Elizabeth (Calendar of State
Papers, Scotland, 1509-1603). They were looked upon
as representing the national feeling, but I doubt much
if any of them had their authorship among the humbler
classes even in the capital, and it is more doubtful still
if they ever found their way into the provinces. At
that time it was comparatively a costly matter to have

a set of verses printed ; and this would make it likely
that those alluded to were composed by persons of
education, a supposition which their pedantic style con-
firms.   For example, in February 1569-70 appeared
several "ballads" in black letter, on the death of the
regent Moray, assassinated by Bothwellhaugh in the
previous month.   One of them thus commenced :—

> Ze montaines murne, ze valayis wepe,
> Ze clouds and firmament,
> Ze fluids dry up, ze sayis so depe,
> Deploir our late Regent.

Compare this with the well-known lines referring to the
treacherous slaughter of the young Earl of Douglas and
his brother, in 1440, when they were dining with the
Chancellor Crichton, and which might have never got
into print but for Hume of Godscroft, who quotes them
in his "History of the House and Race of Douglas and
Angus," written in the reign of James VI.   They are
manifestly an outburst of righteous indignation by some
provincial ballad maker.   "It is sure," says the author
referred to, "the people did abhor it, execrating the
place where it was done, in detestation of the fact, of
which the memory remaineth yet to our days in these
words :—

> Edinburgh Castle, town and tower,
> God grant thou sink for sinne !
> And that even for the black dinner
> Earl Douglas got therein."

Take another illustration from the same source. Godscroft says in connection with his account of the battle of Otterburn,—" The Scots song made of Otterburn telleth the time—about Lammas—and the occasion—to take preys out of England ; also the dividing of the armies betwixt the Earls of Fife and Douglas, and their several journeys, almost as in the authentic history. It beginneth thus :—

> It fell about the Lammas tide,
> When yeomen win their hay,
> The douchty Douglas 'gan to ride,
> In England to take a prey."

Had other writers of the time found the popular songs and ballads to lie as much in their way as the author just quoted did, they would have made similar allusions to them. Neither of the above verses thus preserved would by itself satisfy the objector's idea of the " ancient style." As little would the following stanzas of an English ballad on the battle of Flodden do so, and yet they are found in the " History of John Winchcomb, otherwise called Jack of Newbery," by Thomas Deloney, printed at London in 1596, and are introduced thus—(I quote from Henry Weber's appendix to his edition of "The Battle of Flodden Field," a poem of the sixteenth century,) " In disgrace of the Scots, and in remembrance of the famous atchieved victory, the commons of England made this song, which to this day is not forgotten by many :—

' King Jamie hath made a vow,
    Keep it weel if he may,
That he will be at lovely London
    Upon Saint James his day.

Upon Saint James his day at noon,
    At fair London will I be ;
And all the lords in merry Scotland,
    They shall dine there with me.

' Then bespake good Queen Margaret,
    The tears fell from her eye,
Leave off these wars, most noble king,
    Keep your fidelity.

' The water runs swift, and wondrous deep
    From bottom to the brim ;
My brother Henry hath men good enough,
    England is hard to win.

' Away, (quoth he), with this silly fool,
    In prison fast let her lye,
For she is come of the English blood,
    And for these words she shall die.

' That day made many a fatherless child,
    And many a widow poor ;
And many a Scottish gay lady
    Sate weeping in her bower.' "

In regard to objections founded on particular expressions in ballads recovered from oral tradition, the
upholders of their antiquity are entitled to say that no
compositions thus handed down, especially such as are

constructed like "Sir Patrick Spens," can possibly escape changes in their progress, and if here and there a word or phrase peculiar to a certain era be found, this may indicate merely the period when the change occurred, and not the original date of the poem. Objections of this sort, therefore, do not call for much consideration ; but I will now meet those which have been stated against the present ballad ; remarking at the same time that they do not apply to all the different versions. The use of the word "faem" as an equivalent for the sea, is taken exception to as suspicious, since "no old poet," it is confidently said, "would so use the word 'foam'—none before the era of Pope." Bishop Gavin Douglas completed his translation of Virgil's Æneid on 22d July, 1513, and in his Prologue to the Twelfth Book are these lines :—

> Some sang ring-sangs, dancis, ledis, and roundis,
> With vocis schil, quhil all the dale resounds,
> Quharcto they walk into their karoling,
> For amourous layis dois all the rochis ring :
> Ane sang "The schip salis over the salt fame,
> Will bring thir merchandis and my lemane hame."

Here we have the expression to which attention is called, occurring in a popular song in common use before the battle of Flodden. I have seen it remarked, however, that it is the elliptical use of "sail the faem," for "sail over the faem," which indicates an authorship not older than the days of Queen Anne. My answer to this objection also shall be an example from an " old poet." One of the " Tales of the Three Priests of Peblis," assigned to the early part of the sixteenth century, describes in homely verse the career of a thrifty burgess, and contains these lines (Sibbald's Chronicle of Scottish Poetry, 1802):—

> " Then bocht he wool, and wyselie couth it wey ;
> And efter that some saylit he the sey."

It tries one's patience a little to find the ancient Scottish people denied the possession of the faculty of poetical utterance which is known to belong to savage tribes,— denied even the privilege of readily expressing their ideas with that brevity of phrase involving what the learned call an ellipsis. Were the Scots in the time of Alexander III. so prosaic and literal in their speech, that the line

> " Our gold was changéd into lead,"—

in the song of lament for his death—must be held to refer to an actual transmutation of metals ? The alchemy of poetry is older by thousands of years than chemical science. Its figurative language is derived from no school of criticism.

For the claim of " cork-heeled shoes," " hats," and " fans" to very considerable antiquity, it is enough to refer to such a book as Planche's " History of British Costume." Even among the ancient Romans cork was put into shoes, in order to protect the feet from water, or to give an appearance of greater tallness to the wearer. The truth is, that more is known about the domestic manners of the old Egyptians than about those of our forefathers in the centuries preceding the fifteenth. I confess my inability to say in what king's reign "feather-beds" were introduced into Scotland, but their use as a luxury among persons of high rank on the Continent is much more ancient than the time of our Alexander III. The allusion found fault with strengthens the supposition that the poem had a popular origin, and that it belongs to a period when the mention of feather-beds was not associated with homely ideas.

We have seen that the assumed "inapplicableness of the story to any known event of actual history" is made one of the grounds for suspecting this ballad. Its genuineness has no necessary connection with the authenticity of its narrative, but I am not alone in thinking that in the latter particular also the objection is too hastily advanced. William Motherwell, I believe, first directed attention to the following passage in Fordun's Scotichronicon as narrating the incident to which the ballad refers. "In the year 1281, Margaret, daughter of Alexander III., was espoused to Eric the king of Norway, and leaving Scotland on the last day of July, she crossed the sea in noble style, accompanied by the Earl and Countess of Menteith, and also by the Abbot of Balmerino, and Bernard de Monte-alto (Mowat), and many knights and nobles.—After the celebration of the nuptials, the said abbot and Bernard, and many other persons, in returning home were drowned."* It is worthy of remark that the eleven stanzas given by Bishop Percy, which the objector thinks so "rounded and complete," although alluding to "our Scots nobles" as sharers of the fate of Sir Patrick Spens, speak of no occasion as in any way accounting for their taking part in such a hazardous expedition. The additional stanzas in Scott's "Minstrelsy" throw some light on this, but not even with their help is the narrative "complete" or intelligible.

> "The king's daughter of Noroway,
> 'Tis we must fetch her hame."

The companions of her voyage required to be of noble

---

* "Desponsata est Margareta, filia regis Alexandri Tertii regi Norwegiæ Hanigow sive Hericio nuncupato ; quæ, pridie idus Augusti Scotiam relinquens, nobili transfretavit apparatu, cum Waltero Bullok, comite, et ejus de Menteth comitissa, una cum Abbate de Balmurinach et Bernardo de Montcalto ac aliis multis militibus et nobilibus.—Post vero nuptias solen niter celebratas, dicti Abbas et Bernardus, et alii plures, in redeundo sunt submersi. Walterus autem comes et uxor ejus cum tota familia de Norweia in Scotiam prosperè redierunt."—(Scotichronicon, Goodall's Edition.) The Earl of Menteith and his Lady had sailed apparently by a different ship.

rank, and the "Scots lords" were thus in their right place. But where did the princess take ship? Was the king of Norway's daughter returning to her native land after a visit to Scotland? Such purposeless trips were not made by ladies in old times. Or was she, for some unexplained object, to be brought from Norway to this country? In the latter case the fair Princess must have gone to her grave in the gurly sea with the Scots lords around her. A circumstance heightening so greatly the tragic interest of the story would certainly not have been overlooked by the ballad-maker. Why, moreover, should the Norsemen be represented as making this loud reproach?—

> Ye Scottish men spend a' our king's gowd,
> And a' our queen's fee.

Jamieson's version has a passage to the same effect, without explaining the reason of the mission to Norway. In ordinary circumstances, the expense of entertaining strangers at court, however burdensome to the reigning king of the country, would not be a drain on the purse of his royal sponse. Turn to Buchan's edition of the ballad, and all is clear :—

> But I maun sail the seas the morn,
> And likewise sae maun you,
> To Noroway wi' our king's daughter,
> A chosen queen she's now.

This stanza explains the obscure expressions in the

other versions. To "fetch hame" the king's daughter is
to take her as a bride to her husband, whose home is to
be hers for the future, and such is still the common
expression. By spending "our queen's fee" the
Norwegian nobles meant to say to the Scots,—"The
tocher your king's daughter has brought to our king
will do him little good if you go on drinking and
driving away at his expense." Sir Patrick's answer to
the lords of Norway (I quote Scott's version), is :—

> " For I brought as much white monie
> As gane my men and me,
> And I brought a half-fon o' gude red gowd,
> Out ower the sea wi' me."

The statement about his having sufficient "white
money" to serve himself and his company has nothing
remarkable in it ; but the boast that he had, over and
above this, carried with him to Norway half-a-peck of
gold, may seem merely a bit of romance. It only
exaggerates, however, the historical fact, supposing the
ballad to refer to the marriage of the Princess Margaret
with King Eric. The contract for the marriage fixed
her dowry at 14,000 marks, a fourth part of which was
to be taken with her to Norway.*

Sir Patrick Spens is not mentioned by the chronicler

---

* The contract, dated 25th July 1281, will be found in
Rymer's "Fœdera." It was stipulated that Margaret should
be crowned queen on her wedding day.

as among those who sailed with the Princess, but there
is no necessity for supposing him to have been one of
the leaders of the noble company. The name of Spens
was not one of mark, and the ballad may be wrong even in
assigning to it a knightly prefix. It represents its hero
as having been appointed, for his nautical skill, to take
charge of the ship, a highly responsible post, especially
in those days, but quite distinct from the guardianship
of the future queen, devolving on parties of more
eminent rank, but in whom the ballad-maker may not
have felt so much interest. There is more difficulty in
regarding the narrative as entirely fictitious, than in
believing that this " grand old ballad of Sir Patrick
Spens," as Coleridge, with a poet's ready appreciation of
its merit, calls it, was originally composed at a period
when the fate of the " ancient mariner" whose shipwreck the unknown minstrel sings, was an event, if not
within the memory of persons then alive, yet a living
tradition among the Scottish people.

II.

A SCOTTISH BURGESS OF THE FIFTEENTH CENTURY.

THE well-known ballad which recites "the brim battel of the Harlaw," numbers among those who fell in the conflict,

> "The gude Sir Robert Davidson,
> Wha provost was of Abirdene."

All modern historians of the event thus mention his name with a prefix denoting knighthood, but apparently with no better warrant than the History of Hector Boece, first published in 1526, where he is classed with the "equites aurati," and the poem just quoted, which bears marks of having been composed long after the occasion it refers to, and of having, indeed, been founded on the narrative of Boece.—(See next Note.)   The more authentic account given by the contemporary author Walter Bower, the continuator of Fordun's Scotichronicon, corresponds with the local records, where Davidson's name frequently occurs, and always in the simplest form, like that of any ordinary burgess.

His name is first met with in 1395, when by the Exchequer Rolls (extracts from which Mr. Joseph Robertson has kindly communicated to me), we find him joint collector, along with William Chalmers, another burgess, of the King's or Great Customs of Aberdeen. His accounts in that character extend from 1395 to 1410. In 1398 (the year with which the volumes of the Council Register of Aberdeen commence), he held office as one of the four bailies. But the accounts of the magistrates for the same year exhibit him in another character, that of keeper of a "Taberna" or wine-dealer's booth, where wine was not only sold but consumed. He was, indeed, a general trader in active business, besides farming certain customs belonging to the town. His accounts as collector of the Royal Customs shew him to have been proxy for various persons of high rank, and empowered to draw annuities or pensions granted to them by the crown out of the revenue. He thus acted for Sir Malcolm Drummond, the first husband of Isabella Douglas, Countess of Mar ; for James Stewart, brother of Robert III. ; and for the ill-fated Duke of Rothesay. The first item now to be quoted from the burgh accounts, represents the future Provost in his character of wine-dealer, and also connects him with a man of higher rank, but one whose fortunes had not yet given him a foot of land to call his own, or distinguished his name with a noble title—Alexander Stewart, a natural son of the Earl of Buchan, (the "Wolf of Badenoch"), and afterwards Earl of Mar, and the leader of the Lowland

army at Harlaw.   Under date 1398 there appear the
following payments by the magistrates, with others of a
similar description :—" In the booth (taberna) of Robert
Davidson, for Alexander Stewart and various neighbours
of the town in various potations, XX[s]. Item, for the
expenses of Alexander Stewart's men who were taken,
V[s]. Item, to purchase a bow, arrows, and sword, for
one of his men, XVI[d]. Item, on account of Alexander
Stewart for wine before Robert Davidson's gate, II[s]."—
(Extracts from the Burgh Accounts, in Spalding Club
Miscellany, vol. v.)   In 1398 the future Earl led
a wild and roving life, having at his command a
troop of Highland katerans, with whose aid, in 1404,
he stormed the castle of Kildrummy, belonging to
Isabella, Countess of Mar, and won, by this lion-like
wooing, a bride and an earldom.   The entries quoted
from the accounts of the magistrates of Aberdeen,
taken along with others which mention Alexander
Stewart as having been entertained with wine in different "tabernæ" in the burgh, illustrate its habitual
hospitality towards persons of note, and also lead to
the conjecture that some understanding, of the nature
of a defensive alliance, existed between the community
and the free-living soldier of fortune.   In the same
accounts we find Robert Davidson mentioned as a
magistrate dispensing a cup of wine to the burgesses in
other "taverns" of the town.

It would occupy too much space to quote one-half of the entries in the MS. Council Register connected with Davidson's career as a burgess, and his business as a general merchant ; but a few examples may be selected, although at the risk of overloading this note with matter interesting only to readers connected with Aberdeen. For a course of years preceding his death in battle, he was tenant of fishings belonging to the burgh, in the rivers Dee and Don, and a lessee of the " small customs," also part of the " common good." In 1400 he was one of forty-four persons " ordanit to mak hankaris (anchors) in the havyn for commune profyt ;" four individuals, including Davidson, being appointed to furnish one each, while the rest, evidently less wealthy, were allowed to do so in parties of three and four. In the following year he was received, in the court of the bailies, as attorney for John Wright, in an action for recovery of 13s. 8d. as fen-duty payable by Fergus Adamson for ground in the Shiprow, next to Davidson's own premises. He was repeatedly in court either on his own account or as surety for others. For instance, in 1400, he sued a party for unwarrantably withholding delivery of a woman's hood or wimple (pepla), valued at two shillings ; and he incurred a fine for not producing Richard Conpar in court. In 1402 he was for the first time Provost, or " Alderman," the title then given to the chief magistrate ; and he was re-elected to the office in 1405, 1407, and 1408. In 1406 he obtained a judicial acknowledgment from Simon Skinner that the latter stood pledged for the sum of twenty-one nobles, as the price of a furred mantle or pelisse (furrura), received by the Earl of Moray from Davidson; and he, in his turn, a year afterwards, publicly undertook to recompense Simon, to the satisfaction of honest men, for the carriage of some hides. His last election as alderman was at Michaelmas 1410. In December following he was the guest of the Earl of Mar, enjoying in excellent company the hospitalities of the princely Castle of Kildrummy. The dais of the great hall was graced by the presence of the lady whom Alexander Stewart, on his return from a campaign with the army of the Duke of Burgundy on behalf of the Bishop of Liege, had brought from Brabant to fill the place of the Countess Isabella, gone to her rest; and perhaps the first cup that went round was pledged to the health of the new mistress of the castle. At the right hand of the host and hostess sat the Bishop of Aberdeen, Gilbert Greenlaw, Chancellor of Scotland, attended by Henry Leighton, then rector of Kinkell, who succeeded him as bishop, and whose mitred and robed effigy lies to this day in the north aisle of the ancient Cathedral of Aberdeen, the great tower of which he founded. There was present at the same board a knight who had been the Earl's companion

in arms at Liege, and who is celebrated in the old
ballad :—

> " Good Sir Alexander Irvine,
> The much renownit Laird of Drum ;
> Nane in his days was better seen
> When they were sembled all and some."

Betwixt him and Robert Davidson, Provost of Aberdeen,
was seated William Chalmers, already mentioned, who
had occupied the same office in former years. A few
months later, many of the stalworth forms that filled
the noble hall lay lifeless on the sod of Harlaw, and
of that number were Irvine and Davidson.* The residence of a powerful baron was a sort of provincial court,
and from the Earl of Mar's character for magnificence of
living, we may be sure that Kildrummy was in its
greatest splendour when Davidson visited it—a con-
trast to the silence and desolation of the castle as it now

---

* My authority for this meeting at the residence of the
Earl is the witnessing clause of a charter by "Alexander
Senescalli, comes de Marr et de Garviauch ac dominus de
Duffle in Brabancia," granting certain lands "cousanguineo
nostro Alexandro de Irwyne militi;" dated "apud castrum
nostrum de Kyndromy decimo sexto die mensis Decembris,
anno domini 1410. Testibus——Gilberto Dei gracia Episcopo
Aberdonensi, cancellario Scotie, Magistro Henrico de Lichtoun
rectore ecclesie de Kynkell, Jacobo Senescalli fratre nostro,
Willelmo de Camera patre et Roberto David, cum multis et
diversis aliis."—(Antiquities of the shires of Aberdeen and
Banff, vol. iv. p. 452.)

stands, with its broken walls and all but obliterated
moat. The good burgess may have gone thither in the
way of business as a merchant, or as an ambassador
from his native town on some matter of complaint or
congratulation, or he may have received a special invita-
tion to spend at Kildrummy " the hallow days o' Yule."
At Christmas preceding he had been a guest of the Earl
at his forest castle of Kincardine, on Speyside.*   The
last notice of him in the burgh register is under date
January 1411, when he again appears in his more
homely character, and it is recorded that he was
judicially summoned by Gilbert Gill to fulfil an obliga-
tion which he had undertaken to provide for the
appearance of the master of a ship called the " Cog."

On the whole, it is very pleasing to find Robert
Davidson thus actively engaged to the last in the
different kinds of trade common in the town, meeting
with his fellow-citizens day by day in business or at
board, and readily affording that assistance to them and
others which his social position enabled him to give.
" Prosperous in all his undertakings, and of a high
courage," as he is described in an entry of his death,
found in the ancient chartulary of St. Nicholas' Church,
where he was buried, he was just such a man as should

---

* He appears among the witnesses to a charter dated at
Kincardine, 24th December 1409.—(Antiquities of the shires
of Aberdeen and Banff, vol. iv. p. 177.)

have led out the burgesses to fight against an invading enemy, " in defence of the town and for the liberty of their native soil," as the same record expresses it. By local writers it is mentioned that the great bell called Laurence, presented in 1351 to St. Nicholas' Church by a burgess of the town, was, before the Reformation, never allowed to be rung or tolled except on the anniversary of Provost Davidson's death, and those of two other persons who subsequently enjoyed the like dignity. The circumstance that I am now writing within the sound of the same old bell is my apology for thus entering with some minuteness into the personal history of an ancient Provost of Bon-accord.

III.

BALLAD OF THE BATTLE OF HARLAW.

THIS ballad was published in 1724 by Allan Ramsay in "The Evergreen, being a collection of Scots poems wrote by the ingenious before 1600."* The most opposite opinions have been given regarding it. One writer, in the beginning of this century, observes :—" It

---

* The piece is somewhat lengthy, but the following stanzas may suffice to make my remarks intelligible :—

" Frae Dunidier as I came through,
    Down by the hill of Benachie,
Alangst the lands of Garioch,
    Great pitie was to hear and see
    The noise and dulesome harmonie,
(That ever that dulefu' day did daw !)
    Crying the coronach on hie,
Alas, alas, for the Harlaw !

" I marvelit what the matter meint ;
    All folks were in a fiery farrie :
I wist na wha was fae or friend ;
    Yet quietly I did me carry.
    But sin' the days of auld King Hary,
Sic slaughter was not heard nor seen ;
    And there I had not time to tarry,
For business in Aberdeen.

*   *   *

is much to be regretted that the literary history of the
ballad is involved in so much obscurity. We possess

> " Great Donald of the Isles did claim
>   Unto the lands of Ross some right,
> And to the Governor he came,
>   Them for to have, gif that he might ; '
> Wha saw his interest was but slight,
> And therefore answered wi' disdain.
>   He hasted home baith day and night,
>   And sent nae bodword back again.
>
>   *   *   *
>
> " Then hastilie he did command,
>   That all his weir-men should convene ;
> Ilk ane weel-harnessed frae hand,
>   To meet and hear what he did mean.
> He waxed wrath, and vowed tein ;
> Swearing he wad surprise the North,
>   Subdue the brugh of Aberdeen,
> Mearns, Angus, and all Fife, to Forth.
>
> " Thus with the weir-men of the Isles,
>   Who were aye at his bidding boun' ;
> With mony mae, with force and wiles,
>   Right far and near, baith up and doun :
> Through mount and muir, frae toun to toun,
> Alang the lands of Ross, he roars ;
>   And all obeyed at his bandoun,
> Even frae the north to southern shores.
>
> " Then all the countrie men did yield,
>   For nae resistance durst they mak',
> Nor offer battle in the field,
>   By force of arms to bear him back.

no copy which can be proved to be a century old, and
yet, if internal evidence may be trusted, we may safely

But they resolved all, and spak',
  That best it was for their behove,
    They should him for their chieftain tak',
  Believing well he did them love.

"Then he a proclamation made,
  All men to meet at Inverness ;
Through Murray-land to make a raid,
  Frae Arthursyre into Speyness :
  And further-mair he sent express
To shew his colours and ensenzie,
  To all and sundry, mair or less,
Throughout the bounds of Boyne and Enzie.

"And then through fair Strathbogie land,
  His purpose was for to pursue ;
And whasoever durst gainstand,
  That race they should full sairly rue ;
  Then he bade all his men be true,
And him defend by force and slight ;
  And promised them rewards enow,
And mak' them men of meikle might.

"Without resistance, as he said,
  Through all these parts he stoutly past,
Where some were wae, and some were glad,
  But Garioch was all aghast.
  Through all these fields he sped him fast,
For sic a sight was never seen,
  And then, forsooth, he longed at last
To see the brugh of Aberdeen.

infer, that, with a few modern alterations, it is the identical song alluded to in the 'Complaynt of Scotland.'"

" To hinder this proud enterprise,
    The stout and mighty Earl of Mar,
With all his men in arms did rise,
    Even frae Curgarf to Craigievar,
    And down the side of Don right far :
Angus and Mearns did all convene,
    To fight, ere Donald came sae near
The royal brugh of Aberdeen.

       *   *   *

" With him the brave Lord Ogilvy,
    Of Angus sheriff principal ;
The Constable of good Dundee,
    The vanguard led before them all ;
    Suppose in number they were small,
They first right boldly did pursue,
    And made their foes before them fall,
Wha then that race did sairly rue.

" And then worthy Lord Saltoun,
    The strong undoubted Laird of Drum,
The stalwart Laird of Lawriestoun,
    With ilk their forces all and some ;
    Panmure, with all his men, did come ;
The Provost of brave Aberdeen,
    With trumpets and with tuck of drum,
Came shortly in their armour sheen.

       *   *   *

" Malcomtosh, of the clan head-chief,
    Maclean, with his great haughty head,

R

(Finlay's Scottish Historical and Romantic Ballads,
1808.)   The "Complaynt," written in 1548, and edited

With all their succour and relief,
    Were dulefully dung to the dead ;
And now we are freed of their feid,
And will not long to come again ;
    Thousands with them, without remeid,
On Donald's side that day were slain.

" And on the other side were lost,
    Into the field that dismal day,
Chief men of worth (of meikle cost),
    To be lamented sair for aye ;
    The Lord Saltoun of Rothiemay,
A man of might and meikle main,
    Great dolour was for his decay,
That say unhappilie was slain.

" Of the best men among them was
    The gracious gude Lord Ogilvy,
The sheriff-principal of Angus,
    Renowned for truth and equitie,
    For faith and magnanimitie ;
He had few fellows in the field,
    Yet fell by fatal destinie,
For he naeways would grant to yield.

" Sir James Scrymgeour of Dudhope, knight,
    Great Constable of fair Dundee,
Unto the duleful death was dight ;
    The King's chief bannerman was he,
A valiant man of chivalric,
    Whose predecessors won that place

by John Leyden (1801), mentions "the battel of the
Hayrlaw" among the "sweet melodious sangs of natural

> At Spey, with good King William free,
> 'Gainst Murray, and Macduncan's race.

> " Gude Sir Alexander Irvine,
>   The much renowned laird of Drum,
> Nane in his days was better seen,
>   When they were 'sembled all and some ;
> To praise him we should not be dumb,
> For valour, wit, and worthiness ;
>   To end his days he there did come,
> Whose ransom is remeediless.

> " And there the Knight of Lawriestoun
>   Was slain into his armour sheen ;
> And gude Sir Robert Davidson,
>   Who Provost was of Aberdeen ;
> The Knight of Panmure as was seen,
> A mortal man in armour bright ;
>   Sir Thomas Murray stout and keen,
> Left to the world their last good-night.

> *   *   *

> " In July, on Saint James his even,
>   That four-and-twenty dismal day,
> Twelve hundred, ten score, and eleven,
>   Of years sin' Christ, the sooth to say ;
> Men will remember as they may,
> When thus the veritie they knaw ;
>   And mony a ane may mourn for aye
> The brim battil of the Harlaw."

music of the antiquité" sung by the shepherds; and Leyden remarks, in his Preliminary Dissertation, that this ancient lyric is "still preserved." Mr. Robert Chambers, on the other hand, speaks of the poem as "rightly suspected by antiquaries to have been a composition of much more recent date (than 1600), if not written by Ramsay himself, or some of his friends"— (Scottish Ballads, 1829). Mr. Aytoun refers to the opinions of Pinkerton and Ritson, who throw the date of the piece back to the 15th century, but he differs from those critics, and expresses "a strong suspicion that we owe the ballad to the author of the 'Raid of the Reidswire,'" a poem having "the same turn of expression, and rhythmical mechanism"—(Ballads of Scotland). This conjecture would, as he remarks, give "an authorship not more modern than the early part of the reign of James VI." So far as the age of the composition is concerned, I am not disposed to differ from Mr. Aytoun. My present object is to shew that the verses were composed by some one who had Hector Boece's "Scotorum Historiae" before him.

Comparing the ballad with the History (Edition 1526,* one is immediately struck with the general

---

* I give Boece's account of the battle, for the sake of comparison,—

"At Donaldus qui amitam Eufemiæ, Alexandri Lesle sororem, uxorem habebat, ubi Eufemiam defunctam audivit, a

coincidence between the narratives, differing as they do
in various particulars from the account of the conflict
given by the contemporary writer Bower, in the Scoti-

gubernatore postulavit ex hereditate Rossiæ comitatum. Ubi
quum ille nihil æqui respondisset, collecta ex Hebridibus
ingenti manu partim vi, partim benevolentia, secum ducens,
Rossiam invadit, nec magno negocio in ditionem suam
redegit, Rossianis verum recipere heredem haud quaquam
recusantibus. Verum eo successu non contentus, nec se in
eorum quæ jure petiverat finibus continens, Moraviam,
Bogevallem, iisque vicinas regiones, hostiliter depopulando in
Gareotham pervenit, Aberdoniam, uti minitabatur, direpturus.
Ceterum in tempore obvians temeritate ejus, Alexander
Stuart, Alexandri filii Roberti regis secundi, comitis Buth-
qnhanicc nothus, Marriæ comes, ad Hairlaw (vicus est pugna
mox ibi gesta cruentissima insignis) haud expectatis reliquis
auxiliis cum eo congressus est. Qua re factum est, ut dum
anxilia sine ordinibus (nihil tale suspicantes) cum magna
negligentia advenirent permulti eorum cæsi sint, adeoque
ambigua fuerit victoria, ut utrique se in proximos montes
desertis castris victoria cedentes receperint. Nongenti ex
Hebridianis et iis qui Donaldo adhæserant cecidere cum
Makgillane et Maktothe, præcipuis post Donaldum ducibus.
Ex Scotis adversæ partis vir nobilis Alexander Ogilvy,
Angusiæ vicecomes, singulari justitia ac probitate præditus,
Jacobus Strimger, comestabulis Deidoni, magno animo vir ac
insigni virtute et ad posteros clarus, Alexander Irrvein a Drum,
ob præcipuum robur conspicuus, Robertus Maul a Panmoir,
Thomas Moravus, Wilhelmus Abernethi a Salthon, Alexander
Strathon a Loncenstonn, Robertus Davidstoun, Aberdoniæ
præfectus. Ili omnes equites aurati cum multis aliis nobilibus

chronicon (Goodall's Ed.), compiled upwards of a
century before the work of Boece, and from the notice
of the same event in John Major's History of Great
Britain (Edition 1521), published a very few years
before the latter work. The two chiefs on Donald's
side, and the eight knights on that of the Earl of Mar,
mentioned in the poem, are precisely those who are
named by Boece, although many other persons of rank
were slain in the engagement, and others are named in
the Scotichronicon, in which record, it may be observed,
as well as in Major's book, the death of only one chief
on the part of the invaders is particularly noted. The
unknown bard agrees with the proverbially fallacious
historian in designating "the Provost of braif Aberdeen"
as of knightly rank (a mistake already pointed out),
and also in reckoning amongst the slain—

> " The gracious good Lord Ogilvie,
>   The sheriff-principal of Angus ; "

the person meant being Alexander Ogilvy of Auchter-
house, hereditary sheriff of Angus, who was not killed
at the battle, but survived till 1423—(Lives of the
Lindsays, vol. i., p. 133). His eldest son, George
Ogilvy, was slain on the field. In the same way,

---

eo prælio occubuere. Donaldus victoriam hostibus prorsus
concedens, tota nocte quanta potuit celeritate ad Rossiam
contendit, ac inde qua proxime dabatur in Hebrides se
recepit."

William Abernethy, "son and heir" of Lord Saltoun,
and mentioned as such in the Scotichronicon and by
Major. is styled by Boece "Wilhelmus Abernethi a
Salthon," and as a matter of course figures in the
poem as—

"The Lord Saltoun of Rothiemay."

Particular sentences and phrases in the ballad even
approach to a translation of Boece's Latin. In the
History, for instance, the Sheriff of Angus is said to be
" singulari justitia ac probitate præditus," while in the
poem he is—

"Renounit for truth and equity."

Sir Alexander Irvine, again, is described in the former
as "ob præcipuum robur conspicuus," corresponding
to—

"The strong undoubted Laird of Drum "

of the ballad writer. I look upon the whole structure
of the piece as reared on the account given by Boece,
with amplifications and ornaments introduced as suitable
to a poem, and with the addition also of a few references
to localities in the north. There is no probability that
the historian's narrative was taken from the ballad.
With all Boece's failings as a writer of history, he would
not have taken his materials from a poem in the vulgar
tongue not having the marks of age. It has been
rather hastily assumed that the lines—

"Since the days of auld King Hary,
Sic slaughter was not heard nor seen,"

must refer to the time of Henry VIII. and Flodden
field (1513), an anachronism too absurd to have been
committed by any one writing with such detail on the
subject of Harlaw. The allusion is probably to Henry
IV. and the battle of Homildon, fought in 1402, and
most disastrous to the Scots. This " King Hary" (so is
the name invariably given in Bellenden's Translation of
Boece) died in 1413, two years after Harlaw, and thus
an anachronism still exists quite sufficient to place the
poem much later in date than that event, apart from
the mistakes already noticed. There was the less reason
for the error as to the fate of the Sheriff of Angus, since
he held, next to the Earl of Mar, the chief command of
the lowland force. I suppose the original Latin of
Boece's History to have been the ballad-writer's text-
book, and not the translation of Bellenden, first published in 1536, which omits the particular expressions
alluded to as rendered into the vernacular of the verse-
maker. He may therefore have been a scholarly person,
and an alumnus, perhaps, of the College at Aberdeen
of which Boece was the first Principal ; at all events a
native of the north country, not unfamiliar with the
district—

> " Frac Curgarf to Craigievar,
> And down the syde of Don richt far."

The specification of such localities is not in favour of a
supposition which would assign the authorship to Allan

Ramsay or some of his friends, or to the same hand that wrote the " Raid of the Reidswire." In any view the poem well deserves its place in our collections, although it is not entitled to the rank of an historical ballad, like " Sir Patrick Spens," but must occupy the humbler position of a " Ballad from Scottish History."